DOWN TH

Another Short Story

Written by

MICHAEL DAVIS

2

Dedicated to Liz

Without whom there would have been no adventure

CHAPTER 1 – COMING HOME

"This isn't quite as glamorous as I was expecting," Spike complained as we sat aboard Zulu.

This was the day we launched the boat I had dreamt of owning ever since I had started sailing. However there were to be no royal guests to name her and no bottle of champagne to break against her hull. The harsh reality of sailing on a tight budget dictated that Zulu had been lifted into a cradle, towed by tractor onto a slipway and then left waiting unceremoniously for the waters of the River Thames to come rushing in and float her. In the meantime Spike and I would have to sit on my new yacht for several hours looking less than dignified as we contemplated what would happen once she was afloat.

I had spent months, no, years, browsing the Internet looking for the perfect yacht. Checking eBay and other second-hand boat sites had become a daily routine I had found myself addicted to. The problem had become so acute that Spike had thoughtfully suggested I should consider getting medical help for my appetite for boat porn.

Then one afternoon in early March I decided to take a trip to a small sailing club I could see on the opposite side of the river from my apartment overlooking the Thames. As I wandered inquisitively amongst the large cruisers standing like beached whales on the concrete area in front of the club house a very serious looking man with a grey beard approached me.

"Can I help you?" he asked suspiciously, apparently assuming I was some kind of boat thief. His mood changed dramatically when informed that I was in fact looking to buy a boat rather than steal one. "My name's Brian. I'm actually selling my boat. It's in the boatyard behind the club," he gleefully informed me.

I was led to an area which resembled what I can only describe as a boat graveyard. Brian the beard's boat looked as if it should have been buried a long time ago! Not wanting to appear rude I endeavoured to look interested as I climbed over the decks well aware that this was not the boat I was looking for. Brian left me to talk with someone in the club house which was when I noticed the pretty little boat next to the rotting corpse I was standing on. Yes, she was old and small but it was apparent that she had been well looked after and there on her hull was a sign indicating she was for sale. I discreetly made a note of the telephone number as Brian returned. I made my excuses and left eager to speak with the owner of Zulu. The name evoked an image of a fearless and majestic warrior, resilient and uncompromising in their struggle for survival. Bearing in mind my passion for cookery and a spot of chess I felt sure this was the yacht destiny had decided to partner me with.

A subsequent telephone call informed me that Steve was a retired merchant navy seaman who liked to switch off from life on the oceans by spending his free time sailing on the Thames. Ironic, I thought to myself. He had recently decided it was time to retire from sailing and was selling Zulu with everything I would need to start my nautical adventures. Steve informed me his arthritic knees were no longer strong enough for the rigours of messing around on boats. Another club member later told me that Steve had lost his confidence after crashing Zulu very publicly in front of the club house.

Having parted with my hard-earned cash I set about preparing Zulu for her launch date. I was soon acquainting myself with the pleasures of antifouling and varnishing. Club members who soon became used to me lying prostrate under Zulu, barely recognisable covered in paint, took pity on me and started asking me into the bar for a drink. The friendly barman asked me which boat I was buying and then laughed at my reply.

"I hope you're not taking her too far. She might not stay afloat that long!" Registering the horrified look of shock on my face he quickly assured me that he was only joking and added that he was sure she was more than seaworthy.

Having obsessively checked the integrity of Zulu's hull on numerous occasions in the following weeks, I now found myself sitting with Spike as Archimedes timeless forces lifted her effortlessly from the cradle. In contrast with the afternoon's idle banter with Spike the transition to the frenetic activity which was now required came as quite a shock. Life jackets were secured, ropes were untied and the engine started as a multitude of unintelligible advice was shouted from the well-meaning club members on the Quay.

"Catch the dinghy rope," one of them shouted to Spike. His clumsy attempt failed and the rope to the dinghy which Steve had generously included in our deal fell elusively in the water. Just as I was wondering how we were going to get to shore at the end of our maiden voyage, Spike squeezed himself between the guard rails and proceeded to lunge desperately at the rope with the boathook he had retrieved from the cabin. Fearing I would lose my crew overboard, I grabbed his life jacket just as he succeeded in securing the rope and pulled it on board. This brought a huge cheer from the on looking crowd who had no doubt concluded it was time to call the coast guard in anticipation of our imminent need to be rescued.

In spite of our near disastrous departure we congratulated each other on a successful launch and celebrated by cracking open a packet of hobnobs. Spike was particularly self-congratulatory having as he said proved his worth as my crew. Personally, I had him down as more Captain Hook's incompetent Smee than Kirk's infallible Spock.

Despite a lack of wind, we hoisted the sails enthusiastically and with our dinghy stuttering in tow progressed slowly towards Zulu's new home.

CHAPTER 2 – SAIL PAST

I've never been a great believer in tradition. Turkey at Christmas, cards on birthdays, X-factor on a Saturday night. I can live without all of them. Some might say that tradition connects us with the past and helps us understand our history. I'd say it's just another tool by which our behaviour is manipulated and controlled. Some might say I'm a miserable bastard. I'd have to agree!

Being part of a small sailing club which has recently celebrated its one hundred and twenty fifth birthday, it's impossible to avoid taking part in some of the time honoured customs which are an integral part of the organisation. These include the duck supper at the end of the sailing season, the annual long-distance race to the Thames's barrier, the new member's afternoon tea and the chaotic sail past to celebrate the beginning of the sailing season. Sail past itself consists of a number of eccentric practices which to the uninitiated could result in embarrassment. How many of these could I fail to observe?

It seemed simple enough. First, recruit a happy and willing crew. Jet, her niece Lettie and boyfriend Frank were at least happy, if not willing. Next, sail past the club with all the other yachts and dinghies whose owners were as enthusiastic as me to sail again after a long winter with only sailing books, charts of exotic future destinations and sailing videos on you-tube to act as an antidote to our land constrained malaise. Finally, drinks with the newly appointed commodore back in the club house, where in his elation at his rise to the pinnacle of the club's hierarchy we hoped he might announce free drinks for the evening ahead.

We had been blessed with good weather by the sailing deities and were enjoying the April sunshine as we hoisted our sails in the gentle breeze. The spectacle of so many boats in a small part of the River Thames was an impressive sight and so in order to get a better view and avoid any possible collisions we sailed to the far side of the river in anticipation of the imminent procession. Unfortunately we had no idea when this would happen or whether there was to be some sort of a signal from the shore to indicate kick-off.

"Maybe they'll wave a flag or fire a cannon," Jet suggested helpfully.

"Or light a huge fire like they did in Lord of the Rings," joked Frank, less intent on being supportive.

In an attempt to distract Lettie from the eternal sins of social media I gave her the responsibility of keeping lookout for the as yet unidentified sign which admittedly we didn't even know was going to happen.

"As well prepared as ever," Jet joked just as all the boats on the other side of the river suddenly turned in one direction and started heading back to the club.

"This is it. Ready about," I instructed my crew. Lettie returned to her phone having declared herself redundant in her appointed duty. As we turned around Frank leapt about the boat, vigorously pulling ropes like a rabid bell ringer. Predictably, Jet remained cool and steered the boat onto a course in the same direction as the rest of the flotilla. I continued to admire the line of yachts on the south side of the river which we were suspiciously not a part of.

"They're all waving at us," Jet pointed out. We all waved back although something told me there was some other more sinister motive for the rather frantic waving and gesturing we could see on the other boats. We crossed the imaginary line leading across the river from the club house and celebrated within the restricted confines of the cockpit with some lively fist punching. Moments later the club's fog horn sounded as the commodore crossed the same line in his dinghy followed by the rest of the boats in a dignified procession.

"Well done, Michael. Looks like we came first," Frank commented as Lettie posted a celebratory selfie on Facebook.

We moored Zulu and were soon back on dry land where Frank was relieved to be able to remove the fireman's lifejacket we had issued him with. This antique I had found on the boat would probably have saved his life had he gone overboard but was so cumbersome he had not been able to turn his head for the previous two hours. Fortunately this had not prevented him from putting in a good shift on Zulu and the unbelievably high visibility properties of the jacket had probably provided a significant navigation aid to aircraft flying up the Thames en route to City Airport.

As other crews joined us in the clubhouse I got the impression some of the head shaking and mocking laughter was directed at my crew who were by now toasting their success with large glasses of wine they had served themselves at the bar. Was I being paranoid? Surely there couldn't have been any secret etiquette I had unwittingly failed to observe during such a straightforward parade. I was about to be put out of my misery by one of the more supercilious members of the club.

"Are you aware that all the club boats are expected to follow the commodore across the club line on the same side of the river?" he asked me, knowing full well the obvious answer to his question.

Later in my dreams I was to reply with some brilliant nautical reasoning behind my deliberate break with the club tradition that would reduce the pompous twit to an apologetic wreck, who would then be too ashamed of his misguided assumption to show his face in the club ever again.

In reality I was quite literally saved by the bell. Jet, with her Chardonnay fuelled lack of inhibition, had made her way over to the large bell hung in the corner which I remembered had intrigued her on several previous visits to the club. All eyes had turned in her direction as she joyfully rattled the bell's clapper against its brass counterpart oblivious to the attention she was getting.

"Now the idiot's partner has rung the bell that only the commodore is supposed to use before he makes an announcement," proclaimed the twit. I could see my membership being ripped up as he spoke.

"Thank-you for that timely introduction, Jet. I would like to take this opportunity to welcome everyone back to the club and hope that the season ahead is a successful one with calm seas and a following wind. Can I also add how refreshing it was to see newer members of the club joining in the sail past this year and adding their own twist to the event."

Wow! The commodore's generous intervention had left my oppressor red faced and open mouthed. I resisted the temptation to suggest he put a sock in it. I joined the rest of my faithful crew while the commodore continued his speech anticipating the numerous unmissable events taking place during the year ahead.

"I'm looking forward to some of those races," Frank said with his eternal eagerness.

"Should I post the dates on Facebook?" asked Lettie.

"And in how many of those events will I be saving your ass again?" Jet quizzed.

"Probably most of them," I conceded as I topped up everyone's wine glass.

CHAPTER 3 – SAILING WITH SPIKE

Time and tide wait for no man. So I was delighted my alarm clock had succeeded in waking me early enough to make my 6am meeting with Spike at the sailing club. As we lowered my dinghy and its contents into the sediment laden water of the Thames, we paused momentarily to admire the calmness of the river's surface as it rushed past as yet undisturbed by the abrasive effects of the wind. There was little time to waste so we kept moving before the tide receded and left insufficient water for our short trip out to Zulu's mooring. We hesitated to break the early morning silence with the deafening roar of the dinghy's engine. In fact we hesitated for some considerable time as both of us tried repeatedly to start the stubborn engine with the pull cord. It eventually spluttered to life and I directed us down the now very shallow channel leading from the club's pontoon.

Out in the deeper water the tide assisted in carrying our inflatable dinghy swiftly down river. Passing the other club boats all dutifully pointing into the ebbing tide we hurried along to the more distant moorings reserved for those of us with less years of membership to boast and reminisce about. Thirty seconds later and our early morning departure appeared highly unlikely. Our temperamental engine had died and refused to start despite the cascade of bad language we subjected it to. Spike prepared to paddle as the tide continued to carry us towards our boat. As Zulu came tantalisingly close Spike's rowing took us just out of reach and I failed miserably to reach out to any part of the boat that I could have hung on to. Spike managed to turn the dinghy around and started rowing frantically in an attempt to get us back to the yacht against the strengthening tide. He was soon turning a frightful shade of coronary red in his valiant efforts but the tide was inevitably winning this battle of strength as we drifted further away from Zulu. I concluded that even if Spike had found sufficient time to consume an entire box of Weetabix before our early morning start I doubted they would have provided him with the reserves necessary to shift our heavy inflatable.

"Head us to the buoy further down river," I advised. Grateful to be given permission to stop rowing against the tide Spike used one paddle to guide us to a disused buoy where I grabbed a short piece of rope hanging from the top.

"There's not enough rope to tie us to. I'll have to hang on. There's a radio in my pocket. See if you can reach it." Spike had just about recovered from his earlier energy sapping exertions but now had the more daunting task of retrieving the radio from a pocket inside my jacket. Had anyone seen us we would have appeared the antithesis of the stereotypical testosterone charged seafarer as Spike unzipped my coat and proceeded to rummage around clumsily.

"What am I looking for?" he enquired.

"Something hard with a rubbery bit on the end," I replied to a horrified Spike who temporarily interrupted his search to confirm I was being serious. After an embarrassing few moments Spike produced the radio with all the theatricality of a magician producing a rabbit from a hat and asked what he should do next.

"I've not had to use it before," I replied apologetically. Thinking inventively, I instructed Spike to, "Switch it to channel sixteen and call for the lifeboat." He dutifully followed my instructions and we waited apprehensively for a response.

After twenty anxious minutes and several more distress calls there was still no reply. Being early, there was still no one at the club to wave to for help and no other boats on the river which might respond to me signalling an SOS distress. This would have probably resembled a dyslexic version of the village people performing their hit single YMCA given my limited knowledge of the correct procedure. My arms were starting to ache considerably from holding onto the rope, when an authoritative voice on the VHF radio interrupted the noise of the water rushing past the dinghy.

"This is the London Coast Guard. What is your situation?" After describing our precarious but less than life threatening predicament we were told to hang on while the coast guard instructed the local lifeboat to come to our assistance.

I hoped the lifeboat crew were aware that this was going to be anything but a routine assignment. After all, we were about five hundred metres down river from their base and only around twenty metres from our yacht. From our unfortunate vantage point we watched the crew as they hurried down their pontoon no doubt to the dramatic accompaniment of the Mission Impossible theme tune.

In what seemed only seconds later the bright red rib pulled alongside us. "Are they wearing life jackets?" queried the voice on their VHF radio.

"Yes," confirmed the lifeboat skipper impassionately, whose features I could not discern under his helmet and tinted visor. We may as well have been wearing Telly Tubby armbands for all the recognition of our sea safety awareness did to diminish the humiliation Spike and I were suffering.

"Did we interrupt your breakfast?" I asked light heartedly in an attempt to disguise the shame I was feeling.

"No, far too early," replied the RNLI volunteer who was tying our dinghy to the lifeboat which had come to our aid. A short, but I would insist a significant, thirty seconds later we were stepping onto Zulu and thanking the lifeboat crew as they headed back for their breakfast grinning cruelly inside their helmets.

Only a single but eventful hour had passed since our arrival at the club so Spike and I readied the boat and we were soon heading down river on Zulu's longest trip to date. We were making slow progress downwind in a gentle breeze so I suggested setting up the spinnaker, a sail I had not used before. Some time later I had finished routing the generous number of ropes where I anticipated they would function correctly. If only spinnakers came with IKEA style instructions!

"Are you sure you want to pull that rope?" Spike asked as I prepared to hoist the sail. As I confirmed my intentions Spike secured himself to the boat with a harness expecting an inevitable capsize as the sail launched the boat into warp drive. However as the sail billowed majestically in the wind tugging the boat gently towards our destination Spike was very soon enjoying making tiny adjustments to the sail for optimum performance.

As the world drifted by, we employed our binoculars to investigate some curious looking rocks on the ever-widening mud banks. These turned out to be a family of seals sunning themselves in the early morning isolation of the Thames Estuary. No 'kiss me quick' hats and knotted handkerchiefs here to our relief. Only mother nature at her finest!

After cautiously negotiating the entrance to the River Medway and contemplating the chances of the explosive laden wreck of the General Montgomery spontaneously exploding as we passed, we motored past the buoy marking the sand spit at the start of the River Swale.

Mooring up amongst the lines of local boats we tidied Zulu's ropes before relaxing in the cockpit to admire the pretty town of Queenborough. Zulu, being a small yacht, is only able to tow a very lightweight dinghy before she handles like a bicycle towing a caravan. Consequently the small tender now tied to Zulu's stern was probably designed to carry two small children rather than the much greater load of Spike and myself. Another disaster seemed inevitable! Nervously we succeeded in spreading our weight in the dinghy and with the benefit of the early evening light and a favourable tide paddled erratically to the town's pontoon.

We pounded the deserted streets of Queenborough like sharp shooting cowboys in a spaghetti western until we stumbled upon a take away selling an unusually eclectic menu of Indian, Chinese, Italian and English dishes. Ordering the house special we were surprised not to be presented with a sweet and sour, biryani pizza. After our epic voyage, we had worked up quite an appetite and eagerly devoured our hearty meal while making the short walk back to a pub conveniently located overlooking the river. Loud music and drunken patrons poured out of the small establishment as we shouted our orders at the bar.

"Hello Spike. What are you doing here?" came a most unexpected welcome from the chef as he emerged from the pub's kitchen smoking a cigarette. I assumed the Isle of Sheppey was exempt from the health and safety laws that the rest of the UK was expected to abide by!

Guy turned out to be an old work colleague of Spikes from the days when they'd both been employed by a large drugs company. Knowing Spike to be currently working in sewage I wondered if they were concerned that neither of their careers appeared to be on an upward trajectory. Guy had just finished his shift for the evening and with the three of us fervently chatting and buying drinks we were soon indistinguishable from the other alcohol impaired customers.

As the live band played its last encore to an appreciative crowd we spilled out of the pub into a warm summer night feeling proud that we were now part of the Sheppey rock scene. Emboldened by the effects of the beer we joked about our imminent perilous journey back to Zulu as we strolled confidently to the end of the pontoon. We lowered our dinghy into the water, climbed in and started paddling while humming the theme tune from Hawaii Five-O.

"Are we nearly there yet?" I asked Spike optimistically as I was unable to see Zulu from my side of the dinghy.

"We haven't left the pontoon yet," he informed me with a hint of desperation in his voice. I realised we were going to have to row like Jason and the Argonauts passing through the clashing rocks if we were ever going to get back to Zulu before morning as there was now a strong tidal flow working against us. Both of us started paddling for all we were worth and as the dinghy rocked precariously I hoped we would not end our evening sobering up in the cold River Swale. A bearded sailor, who we had no doubt woken with our confused shrieks of terror and elation, peered at us suspiciously through the gloom from the safety of his cabin's porthole. He continued to watch us with bewildered fascination as we headed uncomfortably close to his shiny new yacht and then on towards Zulu.

Miraculously we pulled alongside our boat just as our chests were about to burst and our arms turn to jelly. We pulled ourselves on board like tag wrestlers dragging themselves back into the ring after both being thrown out by their opponents. Relieved but temporarily paralysed with exhaustion we sat in the cockpit for a while admiring the clear night sky and hypnotic reflection of the town lights in the water. Without the luxury of running water on board we conceded to the fact we would be remaining sweaty for the night and crawled into our cold sleeping bags in the restricted but cosy confines of the bow of our boat.

We both woke early the next morning and hoped no one was watching as we relieved ourselves from the side of the boat.

"Maybe you should consider getting a boat with running water and a toilet," Spike suggested helpfully as we released the ropes from the mooring buoy and headed back towards the Thames.

"Maybe you should go halves with me so we can upgrade to an Abramovic super yacht," I replied, and with Spike contemplating this costly proposition, we headed home.

CHAPTER 4 – OPEN DAY

"Is your boat a long way down the river? It looks really tiny."

I tried to disguise my injured pride. "Actually, it's a small yacht," I retorted indignantly. "Would you like to go for a sail in her?"

"Maybe I could try one of those bigger boats." My ego continued to deflate.

It was the sailing club's open day. An event when it was hoped that hundreds of local sailing muggles would visit and be taken for a spin on a dinghy or cruiser with the expectation that a small percentage would be sufficiently inspired to take up some form of sailing. However, after falling in love with the idea of joining the club and shelling out thousands of pounds on a boat, they would then discover the club was without the mooring facilities to cater for more than a handful of additional yachts. Encouraging new members also presented another tricky conundrum. While financially beneficial it would inevitably lead to the club feeling less exclusive. Less like a nuclear family and more like an extended one with relatives no one cared to remember.

Despite the love of my life Jet, having other plans for our Sunday afternoon, I felt obliged to offer my services taking prospective members out on Zulu. Having convinced Jet to pop by and see how I was getting on later in the day I had arrived at the club alone and eager to impress. Having lowered my dinghy into the water in readiness for transporting eager customers to my yacht I then parked my dinghy trolley next to a table adorned with carefully chosen literature about sailing. 'Knots for Nerds' looked like a particularly compelling read.

"You can't leave that trolley there. Someone will trip over it!" Nodding to confirm my intention to rectify my mistake I decided to ignore the request of one of the club's more officious members as soon as they disappeared to tell someone else what they were doing wrong. Stubbornly I left the dinghy where it was, convinced that only a complete idiot could possibly fail to avoid a collision with it.

With only a handful of visitors and quite a few larger cruisers already in action it appeared Zulu and I were temporarily redundant. I speedily introduced the visitor with over ambitious super yacht aspirations to the club member allocating visitors to boats; a match-making task which he was apparently relishing armed with clipboard and life jackets in an array of sizes and colours. Having relinquished all responsibility for canvassing new recruits I proceeded to the club's galley and consoled myself by over indulging in the tea and cake being offered by some of the female members of the club.

"I have a couple who want to be taken out on a dinghy," the clipboard asked the club's dinghy instructor who was sitting next to me enjoying a generous slice of Victoria sponge. Taking a long, thoughtful look at his watch was not the response clipboard had anticipated. "They already have buoyancy aids on," he added hopefully, with a hint of frustration in his voice.

"I'll take them out," I ventured helpfully. This outburst took me by surprise as much as my companions who were now studying me suspiciously. "I did a lot of dinghy sailing before I joined the club," I offered optimistically. "I'd love the opportunity to sail one of the Wayfarers." Whether it was correctly naming the design of the club's three dinghies or the instructor's continuing concern with the time, I'll never know.

"Great, get yourself kitted up and meet me on the pontoon as soon as possible." Clipboard sounded nervously relieved to have been offered a solution to his dilemma as I hurried to prepare myself for action. With adrenalin pumping uncontrollably round my body, I jumped into the dinghy and tried to recall which ropes controlled which parts of the boat. I reassured myself that my virgin crew would probably turn out to be extreme adrenaline junkies who would appreciate the bumpy ride my limited recent experience was about to subject them to.

"Are you coming on the boat, Arthur?" the slim, woman clearly past retirement age asked the frail pensioner hobbling along the pontoon after her.

"No, I won't make it into the boat," he resigned. I doubt if you'll make it back to the clubhouse without your Zimmer frame, I thought rather disrespectfully as he shakily waved his partner on encouragingly. Florence was an elderly but sprightly blond wearing a pink mohair top. She had no doubt been gorgeous when she was younger and exuded the confidence which comes from having been adored by a great many admirers.

After the obligatory polite introductions and some basic safety instruction my unsuspecting crew was sat nervously in the front of the dinghy oblivious to what was to come. "This is wonderful. It's so exciting." Flo's exultations were cut short as the wind suddenly got stronger and the boat picked up speed, heeling over dramatically. "Slow down, what's happening?" Intent on not being the first club member to give a visitor a heart attack I managed to slow the boat down before the mohair had taken too much of a soaking.

"Should I take you back to the pontoon?" I enquired sympathetically.

"No, this is far too much fun. Keep going!" Florence's emotions continued to swing between unbridled pleasure and utter terror for the next thirty minutes until an approaching safety boat brought our brisk sail to a conclusion by signalling that the open day was coming to an end. Later I was rewarded with the news that while I was de-rigging the dinghy Florence had been entertaining everyone in the clubhouse with tales of her impromptu sailing adventure.

When Jet showed up a little later I could tell immediately she had no intention of doing any sailing. Dressed as she was in tight fitting shorts and a low-cut top she immediately drew admiring glances from the male members of the club and a few disapproving ones from some of their wives. Oblivious to all this attention, Jet continued her conversation on her mobile phone while carrying a chocolate cake precariously in one hand and a bottle of bubbly under her arm.

Simon, who I recalled had been distracted by Jet's charms on several previous occasions rushed heroically to be of assistance. Dropping the rope he had been demonstrating knot tying with to several bored teenagers he ran across the front of the club house, tripped over my irresponsibly abandoned dinghy trolley and ended up head first in the Thames. Despite his wife suggesting otherwise the safety boat retrieved the slightly embarrassed and very wet Simon from the river before hyperthermia set in. Arguably his dampened spirits were improved greatly after he returned with a change of clothes as Jet offered him a glass of her chilled champagne and a slice of her irresistible chocolate cake.

CHAPTER 5 – SAILING SOLO

I stood on the bow of my new boat full of tentative excitement and nervous apprehension. If I detached the lines from the mooring buoy now there would be no turning back. Bridges would have been burnt and gauntlets would have to be run! Now this may all seem a little melodramatic but it was the first time I had taken Zulu out alone. Jet had stood me up and arranged to rendezvous with some of her friends at the cinema to watch Fifty Shades of Grey. This was also a source of much consternation. Spike was at the zoo with his family or had he likened his family to a zoo during our earlier phone call! My memory failed me! Everyone else I had text were all suspiciously otherwise engaged.

As the ropes sank in the murky water I manoeuvred myself carefully from the exposure of the foredeck to the relative security of the cockpit as Zulu started to drift back gently with the tide. I motored carefully away from the other club yachts and headed up river.

My next challenge was hoisting the sails solo. With tiller wedged precariously between my legs I succeeded in raising the mainsail by pulling the main halyard while steering the boat in something resembling a straight line. Had the coastguard been monitoring my progress they would have no doubt concluded that I had been over indulging in the club bar before my excursion. With the mainsail set I unfurled Zulu's genoa, and as she gracefully ploughed through the water I relaxed and took in the diversity of my surroundings. The lower Thames may be flanked by an ever-changing backdrop of untamed wilderness, industrial landscape and modern housing estates but this lends it an unpredictable charm which is mesmerising. Before the river had completely hypnotised me, I was bought back to reality by a rumble of nearby thunder. I cursed the Met office who had failed to warn me of this on their weather app. Fortunately, I was close to the sailing club where I had purchased Zulu and I headed for the shelter of this sanctuary as hastily as I could.

After quickly bringing down the sails in a very untidy fashion I approached a mooring buoy, snagged it with a hook from the safety of the cockpit and finally pulled myself up to the buoy from the bow. Just as I crawled into Zulu's snug cabin the heavens opened as a squall passed over bringing with it strong winds which whipped up waves that crashed into the boat's topsides sending salty spray across the decks. Survival instincts kicking in I put the kettle on and tucked into a packet of custard creams. With the radio playing Queen 'We are the Champions' I prepared myself mentally for the impending test of my endurance. I imagined Scott indulging in similar emotions as he raced across the Antarctic.

Twenty minutes and half a packet of biscuits later the storm passed over and the sun's reappearance prompted me to venture cautiously back on deck. The sea can be such a cruel mistress, I pondered as I registered the dramatic transformation of the Thames. With the wind having dropped, the water was now almost mirror like in its tranquillity.

I text Jet to inform her I had survived the storm. I pictured her sat distraught in a dimly lit bar with other concerned sailor's partners watching the news for information concerning their loved one's safety. Unlike Clooney I had weathered 'The Perfect Storm' and would be duly reunited with my loved one.

"That's good. Has there been some bad weather?" Her reply suggested that from the comfort of a warm cinema seat in an air-conditioned theatre the passing rainstorm may not have seemed quite so perilous.

Starting the engine and detaching myself from the buoy, I motored back down the becalmed river towards my home sailing club. The ebbing tide was now running fast as I used the same technique to hook the buoy from Zulu's cockpit. Pleased with myself for the efficiency of my solo mooring strategy I stepped onto the side deck just as the buoy disappeared under the boat. Summoning the strength of Hercules, I pulled on the rope but in vain. The buoy was caught between Zulu's twin keels and was now turning her beam onto the tide. This caused her to heel over dramatically, forcing me to hang on to the guardrail as I steadied myself on the bow of the boat. What I would give for an extra crew member, I thought to myself. Not that an extra pair of hands would have made getting out of this predicament any easier but sharing the experience would have made the situation much less distressing. All is not lost yet! Robert Redford endured far more serious misadventures when his boat was holed by a shipping container in the middle of the Indian Ocean. Moving back to the cockpit, I tried putting the engine in forward and reverse at full throttle but Zulu was stuck fast.

Resisting the urge to jump overboard, Forest Gump style, and swim the short distance to shore I accepted the inevitability of another lifeboat rescue. Familiar with the routine I called the London Coastguard and within minutes heard the lifeboat engines roar to life a few hundred metres up the river. Would I be able to collect points towards a free gift I mused as I anticipated another embarrassing explanation to the RNLI crew?

The three people on the bright orange rib comprised an older, ruddy faced skipper who appeared to be training a couple of younger, inexperienced recruits. After a lot of shouting about how they were going to proceed, the skipper brought the lifeboat alongside Zulu and one of his team clambered onto my boat. After some unnecessarily polite introductions, a tow rope was attached to a cleat at Zulu's bow. The malevolent buoy was to prove no match for the lifeboat's powerful engines and within seconds I was contemplating mooring up less dramatically and taking the short dinghy ride back to the clubhouse bar. However, the lifeboat crew had other intentions. Another heated discussion ensued as to the correct procedure to follow now that the initial rescue had been successfully completed. I was grateful that I had not been an injured casualty in need of urgent medical attention as the training manual the recruits had recently digested did not appear to agree with the methods preferred by the skipper. Eventually they insisted on towing me upriver, tying Zulu to a more substantial mooring buoy before taking me back to shore. I thanked them sincerely as they sped off down the river, voices raised in perpetual disagreement. Hopefully I would not make an appearance on a future episode of 'Saving Lives at Sea.' As I walked the short distance back to the club house I contemplated the retrieval of both Zulu and my dinghy which were now moored to separate buoys beyond my reach out in the river.

I may now have appeared a little over cautious dressed as I was in a full set of red waterproofs I had changed into earlier while waiting for the rain to stop. By the time I reached the clubhouse I was in danger of dehydrating inside my very well insulated sailing attire. The few members who were still busy at the club looked on in disbelief as I hastily ripped off several layers of clothing as soon as I was back on dry land. To their great relief I stopped undressing before I could cause any embarrassment and headed to the bar for some urgent liquid refreshment and the opportunity to tell some fellow mariners about my inaugural solo sailing adventure. After a few drinks I anticipated it would be more likely that some generous soul would offer me a lift back to my dinghy.

Fortunately the club is full of sailors eager to give advice and help out and after marvelling at yet another of my tales of near disaster Clive ferried me back to Zulu in the dinghy he had recently acquired and lovingly restored. He kindly advised me not to advertise the fact I had called out the lifeboat again although he couldn't promise that the dozen or so members who had witnessed my latest rescue wouldn't be tempted to share the story at the next club function. I thanked him and promised to buy him a drink later as I stepped aboard Zulu. I motored back to my allotted buoy and moored up from the bow to avoid a repeat of my earlier mishap. Finally able to dinghy back to shore and head home I tried not to imagine how my reputation could be ruined any further.

CHAPTER 6 – FANCY DRESS

"Are you sure about the eyeliner?" I ventured nervously.

"It'll be fine," replied Jet, not too convincingly as she tortured my eyelids with her applicator. I could tell she was enjoying turning me into a rather weather-beaten version of Jack Sparrow by the sadistic smile on her otherwise angelic face. What was baffling me was how I had allowed myself to be talked into this gruesome makeover knowing it would lead to inevitable humiliation.

Several weeks earlier the conditions had been perfect for sailing. A steady, warm, southerly breeze and a cloudless sky had enticed me down to the club despite having no one to sail with. I had struggled to load my dinghy onto its trolley and dragged it clumsily round to the club's crane. This was operated regularly to lower dinghies into the water, which everyone used to get to their yachts moored in the river. I placed the two ropes attached to my dinghy on the crane's hook and pressed the button to take her up. Bang! The crane stopped abruptly as I stood motionless, shocked by the unexpected interruption to a task I had undertaken countless times.

My first thought was to look around to see if I could spot the sniper who was taking pot shots at me. Had I upset Jet so much by refusing to take part in her re-enactment of scenes from Fifty Shades of Grey that she felt inclined to respond in such an extreme manner. I quickly brushed such chilling ideas aside as I noticed the curious angle at which the crane was now tilted. Now my thoughts turned to what I had done to cause the damage followed

35

by the realisation that my perfect day's sailing could well be ruined. I pressed the control button a few more times in desperation but there was no response.

As I despondently removed my dinghy from the crane, my old friend, Kevin strode purposely through the gate of the club looking in need of a drink.

After a quick assessment of the situation he concluded cheerfully "You're lucky to be alive. This was an accident waiting to happen. The crane could have easily collapsed on top of you. You'll be needing a large brandy to get over the shock." The club's small but well stocked bar was subsequently opened and the appropriate remedy administered.

It turned out that several of the bolts holding up the crane had severely rusted and were already broken prior to my attempted excursion. I felt vindicated that the demise of the crane had not been a result of my incompetence but there still remained the problem that without the crane the only way for anyone to get to their yacht was a cold, perilous swim in the Thames.

Procuring the substantial amount of money to replace the obsolete crane was going to take some serious fund raising. The entertainment committee would have to be alerted to the situation and tasked with resolving the crisis. A mission verging on the impossible! I hoped Clive Davison, the club's answer to Tom Cruise, would prove his worth as the committee's chair. A raffle would definitely not generate enough cash; a sponsored run would probably wipe out half the club while a barn dance meant the inevitable horror of cowboy boots and chequed shirts.

So here I was resembling a camp Captain Blackbeard sporting a billowing, oversize woman's blouse, an orange and silver gown which could have given Joseph's technicolor dreamcoat some stiff competition and a long, dark wig complemented by a bright red bandana. Predictably Jet looked almost edible in her short grey dress with laced bodice, stockings and provocative thigh high boots, long purple gloves and makeup and jewellery which looked as if they could grace a Hollywood film set.

Dam Clive for organising a pirate's fancy dress! Even the idea of a toe tapping, dosey doeing barn dance seemed more appealing as we drove the short distance to the club. Jet looked confused when I insisted that she drove, watching bemused as I crawled into the back seat and hid myself on the floor behind her.

It was one of those rare late summer evenings when the temperature is just warm enough to sit outside. Many of the club members were making the most of this and were enjoying the view of their boats dutifully lined up as the sunlight danced hypnotically on the water.

I noted with relief that Clive and his girlfriend had made a similarly bold effort with their costumes. However, most of the others seemed to have shared out the contents of one person's costume draw between them. An eyepatch here, a neckerchief there and a couple of ill-fitting pirate hats thrown in for good measure. Some apparently seemed to think that groaning "Ou ar me hearties," at regular intervals would somehow distract from the fact they looked more like a poor man's village people than a crew of angry pirates. Ignoring the questioning looks my extravagant costume and heavy make-up were drawing I headed inside to get a much needed drink from the bar. As we waited for our very tropical rum cocktails to be shaken Jet whispered in my ear that she seemed to be getting a few disapproving looks from some of the women who had dressed as slightly more conservative pitratesses.

"What have you got on your crane-ium?"

"Have you sailed from waters afar? Maybe the U-crane." I quickly realised I was going to be the butt of some pretty awful jokes during the evening having had the misfortune to have been operating the focus of the fundraiser when it had broken.

After taking a good deal of light hearted ribbing we were asked to take our seats at the neatly arranged tables as dinner was about to be served. Having expected well-preserved dried biscuits and scurvy repressing oranges and bananas I was pleasantly surprised at the delicious fayre being dished up. After washing down the generous helpings of sausage and mash with copious amounts of refreshing grog it was time to get into teams for the much anticipated seafaring quiz. Jet cunningly teamed up with a delighted Kevin who reputedly had an encyclopaedic knowledge of just about everything nautical while I was grabbed by a couple who had recently joined the club.

As Jet revelled in writing down the answers Kevin confidently whispered in her ear, my team were struggling to comprehend the idea of a quiz based solely on sailing.

"I'm sure we'll do better on the literature and history rounds," Vanessa suggested optimistically to her husband Andy.

"I do hope you have a good knowledge of music, Michael. Vanessa and I are tone deaf." Had I really teamed up with the quiz team from hell?

Despite Jet's rather mercenary approach to the evening's light-hearted entertainment she was astonished when beaten into second place by a team who looked as if they had sailed all of the seven seas and discovered a few more along the way. Her disappointment was further compounded when I was announced as the best dressed pirate for which I was presented with a very large bottle of expensive looking rum.

Although it was getting late and most people were starting to leave it seemed rude not to open the bottle and share it with everyone. When the winners of the quiz opened their bottle of whisky, it was clear that the small crowd of pirates remaining were in for a long night. By the time we left and said our farewells to some of the more hardy pirates who were crawling into their boats for the night I realised what good friends I had found at the club. As the miraculously sober Jet drove us safely home with the prospect of several hours of painful makeup removal ahead of us she confided that she also felt that she had been accepted and welcomed in a way she had not been before.

CHAPTER 7 – COASTAL SKIPPER COURSE

"Congratulations! You've passed the coastal skipper practical course. You kept the boat safe at all times and picked up the techniques I showed you quickly."

"Thank-you. I know we haven't got on this week but I have learnt a lot and for that I'm grateful."

It had been a long and eventful five days sailing up the east coast and back, and joining the crew the previous Sunday seemed a lifetime ago.

I had been the last to arrive and descending the companionway I found myself jammed in the training yachts small saloon with the four strangers I would be spending most of the next week sailing with. Geoff was also taking the coastal skipper course while Alice and Keith were there as competent crew.

Harry, the instructor, suggested we unpack and then meet in a nearby pub for dinner. As we had all accepted living out of a bag for the week and didn't feel there was much point in unpacking it was not long before formal introductions were being made over a warm meal. Geoff owned a forty-one foot yacht which he kept in Brighton marina. Impressive! Even more so when he later confided to me it had electric winches, an electric toilet and was set up to make life afloat as simple as possible. He may have regretted showing me the photographs of his super yacht as I was unable to resist teasing him at every opportunity during the forthcoming trip. In stark contrast, Alice and Keith had recently inherited a boat at the other end of the seafaring scale. Their small yacht would probably have fitted into one of Geoff's cabins and still have left room for his snooker table. Keith had dinghy sailed in the past while Alice had no experience of sailing but was willing to, "Give it a go." After a couple of drinks I may have overestimated how interesting my entire life story was. Eventually noticing Geoff yawning and Keith snoring, having fallen asleep on Alice's shoulder, I concluded my tale with an optimistic "I'm looking forward to the challenge."

After an unsociably early start the next day I was tasked with skippering the yacht through the marina lock and into the River Medway. After reversing away from our pontoon, I motored slowly into the lock with my crew poised with ropes to tie us up. As the yacht came to a gentle stop Keith stepped off nimbly and secured the bow line but like a horse, not quite sure of its rider's equestrian ability, Alice froze. As the boat's stern began to drift into the middle of the lock Harry reacted instinctively and lassoed a cleat on the lock's pontoon. We were now secure as I contemplated if this was a sign of things to come.

With very little wind, we motored to our first destination with Geoff and myself using the charts to give instructions to Alice and Keith on the helm, on how to get there. Arriving at Queenborough early in the afternoon, we practiced mooring up to pontoons in the river giving Alice an opportunity to practice jumping on and off the boat. She quickly mastered this and given a cutlass and musket could have easily been mistaken for a pirate boarding a Spanish galleon packed with treasure. Despite this improvement I couldn't help noticing our instructor's frustration when someone hesitated or got something wrong. Surely having your head in your hands when a knot was tied incorrectly was not the best way to motivate and encourage your crew?

Later in the evening we went ashore while our instructor opted to stay on the boat on the pretext of recording our progress so far. Along the shorefront were several benches one of which had a plaque with the message 'Happy to chat'. We considered the numerous amusing implications of this but were pleased to see the primary school buddy bench idea had evolved into adult form.

The first pub we encountered had already closed which sent an apprehensive chill through our bodies which were desperate for something to remedy the rigors of a testing first day. Fortunately we soon stumbled on a backstreet micro pub which looked promising with its brightly lit interior obscured through steamed up windows. As we entered the busy establishment everyone turned to look at us. I'd seen American Werewolf in London. Was this Kent's equivalent of the Slaughtered Lamb? Ours fears were quickly allayed as one of the men sitting on stools around the bar smiled at us warmly and said "It's quiz night. If you've got half a brain cell between you, you can join our team." Despite our limited contribution to the success of the rather unoriginally named Bar Stewards the locals continued to be hospitable and when we finally made our way back to our boat we did so with some fond memories.

The next morning Keith emerged from the cabin he was sharing with his wife Alice in a pair of very conservative tartan pyjamas. I laughed and commented on how I admired what a refreshingly traditional guy he was. He then confessed that Alice had insisted he pack nightwear that would not only keep him warm but ensure he did not expose too much naked flesh. I pointed out that I thought the rest of the crew would probably have been able to resist him even if he'd surfaced wearing a pair of budgie smugglers. Geoff nodded in distasteful agreement.

Today was Geoff's turn to skipper the boat and navigate the challenging Thames estuary. Despite being advised by Harry to spend eighty percent of his time on deck advising the crew he appeared to be chained to the chart table checking our position and subsequent heading. This was not helped by the fact that Harry had a habit of interrupting him in the middle of each task to give a lecture on how to do the job properly. Was this a pre-planned test of our ability to work under pressure or was our instructor just a bit self obsessed? Eight hours later we arrived safely at the pretty Essex town of Brightlingsea and after an unexpectedly hearty meal prepared by Alice and Keith I set to work planning the next day's passage.

Having not washed for two days we were all keen to go ashore the next morning to use the showers. After agreeing we would leave Brightlingsea at nine o'clock a water taxi picked us up and during the short journey to land I quizzed the harbour master how to negotiate the shallow channel out of the harbour. Surely using local knowledge could not be seen as cheating. I swore the others to secrecy as our instructor had chosen to remain on the yacht and was unaware of my 'insider trading'.

We were relieved to discover the local sailing club's showers were open and while Alice enjoyed the luxury of having the lady's facilities to herself Geoff, Keith and I were forced to share the one shower we discovered in the gents. A considerable period of time passed while we each took our turn revitalising ourselves in the hot water. We were probably quite fortunate to find the harbourmaster still waiting for us at the end of the pontoon when we eventually rejoined Alice. After we had explained why we had taken so long he kindly informed us that had we opened the door at the back of the toilets we would have found another three shower cubicles. We groaned as we were dropped off by the harbourmaster who must have been wondering how we were going to navigate the Thames estuary having been unable to find our way round a public convenience.

Harry summoned me to the cockpit while the rest of the crew busied themselves tidying up the boat.

"So what's your plan for departure?" he asked.

"Well due to the unfortunate delay we'll leave at nine thirty and…."

"No, no, no, no, no!" he interrupted unexpectedly. "You said we would leave at nine and now you're changing your mind. You can't skipper a boat like this."

I'd had enough of this. I'd politely listened to him undermine Geoff the previous day and had no intention of being treated the same way.

"We can't leave at nine. We couldn't help being so long in the showers," I explained slightly inaccurately. "A skipper has to be able to adapt when circumstances change." Harry was starting to go red in the face, unable to hide his irritation.

"Do you really believe the way you're behaving is the best way to motivate your students?" I added. "Surely you should be modelling how a good skipper encourages his crew with patience and professionalism."

This was too much for Harry. He stormed off down the companionway, slamming the hatch which almost severed Keith's fingers and proceeded to slam the door to his cabin.

"What's wrong with you?" I shouted after him in complete disbelief at what I had just witnessed. Geoff looked at me supportively while Alice and Keith looked to be in a state of shock. Harry resurfaced with his phone and without speaking to anyone stepped off the boat onto the pontoon. Marching up and down like a caged animal we could overhear his conversation with the company who owned the boat. After much gnashing of teeth it became apparent that he was begging his boss to send someone to replace him but without success.

Eventually he appeared to calm down and rejoined the rest of us who were now sitting in the cockpit drinking hot beverages.

"Cup of tea?" Keith asked in a much more conciliatory gesture than I would have been able to manage at that particular moment. Having accepted the kind offer Harry informed us that there was no one who could take over from him and that he was stuck with being our instructor for the rest of the week. However we were free to make our own way home if we were not happy with the arrangements.

"That's good," I replied resolutely, "because I have no intention of getting off this boat until I've completed the course." The others agreed that they wanted to continue and we left Brightlingsea with the conversation marginally less convivial than the previous day.

It was a gloriously warm and sunny morning but with very little wind we had no choice but to head out of the Blackwater estuary under engine. This did make planning the course back to the River Medway much simpler so Harry, not unreasonably, instructed me to plot a course which took us much further out into the English Channel. By now I was determined not to give him any excuse to find fault in my sailing knowledge so I promptly sat at the chart table and used the available resources to work out a course to steer. Emerging confidently from the saloon I gave my instructions to Alice who was enjoying helming the boat and positioned myself at the rear of the cockpit where I could monitor our progress while initiating some light-hearted banter with the crew.

It was a long way back to Queenborough using the engine and later in the afternoon it became apparent that we would be completing the last part of the voyage in the dark. I set to work consulting the charts while Alice and Keith nervously questioned Harry as to the hazards of sailing at night. As dusk approached Geoff generously offered to start preparing a meal we could enjoy on arrival while the rest of us kitted up in our warmest sailing gear. Armed with headings and light sequences Alice and Keith were soon busy identifying the flashing lights on the buoys guiding us towards our destination. I was relishing helming the boat and instructing my crew using the plan I had earlier prepared. With huge ships passing close by in the Thames estuary and the billions of stars above us to accentuate how small and vulnerable we were on our modest yacht, we started to experience the thrill of adventure that all pioneers who push themselves beyond their comfort zone must feel. As we moored up alongside our pontoon we felt both a sense of elation and pride at our accomplishment. We were also relieved to end the journey in one piece with a hot meal waiting for us down below. How Geoff had managed to prepare the gourmet meal he presented us with, in a tiny galley on a rocking boat I will never know.

After the meal Harry offered to wash up so the rest of us could go for a drink. Retiring to the sociable micro pub we soon found ourselves discussing the day's events and agreed that although we shared concerns over our instructor's style of teaching he had made amends by sharing his knowledge and love of sailing with us during the journey. It had been a long and intensive day and a couple of drinks, which continued to bond the friendship between the four of us, were all we could manage before we felt the call of our beds back on our boat.

The next day Harry promised to put us through our paces but first Alice and Keith, as part of their competent crew course, would be learning how to row a dinghy safely. Sensing a great photo opportunity, I readied myself with my camera, anticipating the moment one of them managed to fall in. Disappointingly, despite a lot of laughter, shrieking and splashing about, both of them passed their lesson with flying colours. Geoff and I were enjoying the spotlight being turned on our two friends but wondered what Harry had in store for us after Alice and Keith had dried off.

We practiced mooring to pontoons for a while which having become familiar with the yacht we both found quite easy and then headed off into the Medway to try heaving to. This is a useful technique for stopping a boat quickly with the sails up and isn't too challenging a manoeuvre. I completed the task a couple of times and handed the helm to Geoff. Harry watched as Geoff started off sailing the boat confidently into the wind. As he continued to sail the boat in a straight line I was literally willing him to act. Eventually when we were getting dangerously close to a large mooring buoy in the river Harry took the helm impatiently and steered us away from the hazard.

"What do you think went wrong?" Harry asked. Geoff was obviously unsure and muttered a few excuses which Harry was obviously not impressed with. I was surprised that without giving any advice Harry asked Geoff to try again. This time I stood out of Harry's field of vision where I was able to help Geoff with some subtle miming of what he needed to do. Geoff managed the technique on his second attempt if a little hesitantly. My instincts told me that Geoff's confidence had been knocked and that Harry was probably aware of the support I had given him.

My next task was to anchor the boat in an almost land locked pool which was approached through a narrow, unmarked channel. Harry offered some advice on the pilotage techniques I might use which although I was familiar with I had not applied before in such a demanding situation. I successfully negotiated the channel with everyone watching apprehensively and with help from the crew anchored in a quite spectacular spot which I promised myself I would visit again on Zulu. We were grateful that Harry suggested we stop for some lunch which allowed us to sit and admire the scenery while feasting on some delicious sandwiches prepared by Alice and Keith.

As we left the pretty anchorage Geoff was given a slightly less challenging spot to anchor in which I felt was a wise decision. As he checked the charts I noticed Harry hurrying him unsympathetically which was turning him into a bag of nerves. Geoff asked me to helm the boat so that he could focus on navigating us to a suitable spot. I was more than happy to do this but was worried that our instructor's insensitive approach had dampened my colleague's spirits. However we anchored successfully and as we headed back to Queenborough Geoff appeared to relax a little.

Before we could become too complacent Harry suggested we try mooring up to a buoy under mainsail alone. Again I was happy to volunteer to go first and using an unfamiliar technique which

Harry explained to us I brought the boat to a stop so that Alice could slip a rope through the ring on top of the buoy. Geoff followed my example and looked pleased with himself as the buoy was similarly snagged.

"It's much more difficult under headsail alone, of course," Harry boasted. "Anyone fancy having a go?"

"Why not?" I said, accepting the challenge. I had now become very single minded in my determination to demonstrate my sailing skills.

"We're starting to drift backwards with the tide," Alice informed me from the bow of the boat. Maybe I had overestimated my abilities. I had instructed Keith to gradually furl in the genoa as we approached the buoy. This had slowed us down but now meant we did not enough power to reach our goal.

"Let the genoa back out a little," I asked Keith who responded quickly and to my relief we started moving forward again. Keith proceeded to pull the genoa back in again but this time Alice was able to attach us to the buoy as the boat came to a stop.

"Well done," Harry offered grudgingly as we released the buoy and motored up the river to where we would spend the night.

After only four days away, the evening followed what appeared to be a familiar routine. Following a hearty meal Harry stayed aboard the boat to complete the paperwork on his mutinous crew while the rest of us headed off to the pub to discuss the day's events.

Even Alice and Keith were unhappy with the way Harry was treating Geoff and pointed out that he would probably have made him walk the plank by now had we lived in a different century. There was now a strong bond between the four of us partly because of our instructor's strange temperament. We all confessed to having mixed feelings about finishing the course the next day. Sad that we would be saying goodbye to each other but relieved to be getting of Captain Hook's not so Jolly Roger. Geoff was concerned that he would not pass the course but was intent on sending a letter of complaint when he got home.

On our final morning we practiced our man overboard technique which regrettably did not involve throwing our instructor off the boat. Instead we had to rescue a plastic fender which Alice and Keith took turns in flinging into the water. Again Harry showed us a different method to the one I was familiar with and I was grateful to learn something new. Geoff and I repeated the procedure several times until Harry appeared satisfied we were unlikely to ever leave a fender drowning in the Medway.

Before we could finish the course we needed to show that we could gybe the boat safely. This involves turning the boat while going downwind and can result in the boom flying across the boat very violently. As knocking one of your crew's heads off their shoulders or causing some costly damage to the yacht was most probably a prerequisite for failing the course I was keen to get this one right. With my crew diligently following the instructions I gave as clearly as possible I completed the manoeuvre a couple of times without any mishaps. Geoff took the helm and headed downwind. Somehow I knew what he was going to do but had no way of preventing it. Instead of turning the stern through the wind he turned the boat further into the wind making the instructions he was giving his crew utterly redundant. Exasperated, Harry asked Kevin to take over the helm, told Geoff to take a seat and then squatted down next to him.

Again the unnecessary Spanish inquisition! "How do you think you could have improved what you just did?" Geoff obviously didn't have any idea but Harry continued to push him while the rest of us sat uneasily.

"I can't listen to this any longer," I insisted. "This is making me feel really uncomfortable. Geoff obviously doesn't know he turned the boat the wrong way and needs advice on what he should have done rather than this continual undermining of his confidence."

Harry turned towards me looking angry enough to make me suspect this could end unpleasantly. Pistols at dawn possibly? "If you feel uncomfortable then go down below," he suggested malevolently.

"I'm not going anywhere!" I replied indignantly. "And if you're not going to support Geoff then I will."

"Can you stop interfering with my course," he ordered allowing me to find a fatal floor in this request.

"This wouldn't be your course if you'd have got your way. You would have abandoned us two days ago if your boss could have replaced you." Had I twisted the knife in a little too boldly?

Harry was lost for words. The wind was picking up and the sound of the flogging sails mercifully filled the uncomfortable silence. Fortunately it was time to head home. Harry retreated to the saloon where he did some final work with Alice and Keith. Geoff and I brought the mainsail down and unfurled the genoa in the strengthening breeze. I made sure it was a swift sail back to our marina where Harry insisted he helmed the boat through the lock.

After we were safely back on the yacht's berth Harry took Geoff to the company's office to debrief him while the rest of us tidied the boat and packed our bags. Thirty minutes passed and Keith, Alice and I looked at each other concerned that Geoff was suffering another interrogation. Eventually Geoff returned alone looking surprisingly upbeat.

"I've not passed but I can join another course later in the year to demonstrate the things I got wrong," he informed us. "Michael, you're up next. Good luck!"

As I walked along the pontoon towards the office Harry met me half way and in a conversation he evidently wanted to keep as short as possible gave me the news that I had passed the course. We joined the others on the yacht where Alice and Keith were informed they had completed the competent crew course successfully. We toasted their accomplishment before heading off to the car park leaving Harry to contemplate the class from hell.

The four of us swapped phone numbers, hugged each other emotionally and shared some final jokes about our unforgettable week.

Much to Harry's misfortune his attitude had been the reason I had found the inner strength which had enabled me to deal with every challenge I had been presented with. I hoped this quality would make me a skipper who would inspire and motivate in the future. I felt certain Jet would be only too quick to let me know if it didn't.

CHAPTER 8 – THE DUCK SUPPER

'Will we get to meet the commandant?' Jet asked inquisitively. Had she really dressed in those jackboots expecting to be dining with the commanding officer from a German prisoner of war camp or was it simply that her knowledge of sailing club hierarchy was still a little sketchy? Assuming the latter I informed her that to the best of my knowledge the club commodore would indeed be attending the annual sailing club duck supper.

This was to be our first opportunity to attend a formal club event and we were unsure what to expect. I had scrubbed up quite respectably with the help of Jet's sympathetic and patient advice and found my best suit so far back in my wardrobe I was close to visiting Narnia. Jet looked stunning in her favourite colour, black, complemented by a tasteful selection of sparkling accessories.

On arrival we headed for the refuge of the bar, grateful to be approached by a couple of familiar club members who immediately made us feel welcome. The club secretary dutifully informed us where we were sitting but everyone continued to make polite conversation in the absence of any bustling waiters keen to take our orders. By the time we were eventually asked to take our seats several of the members were already virtually incoherent and I whispered to Jet that the evening possessed all the ingredients necessary to ensure it was likely to become anything but boring.

Eventually, and to my mind well overdue, the hor d'oeves were served. I had been concerned for some time that several more portly guests had a distinct look akin to Hannibal Lecter before ordering a large glass of Chianti.

As good food and fine wine arrived at our tables polite conversation became more relaxed and jovial. Taking me unawares I almost choked on a cranberry as the Master of Ceremony unexpectedly banged his gavel loudly on the table and addressed the gathering very formally.

"Please be up standing for Grace." We dutifully obeyed and were only instructed to sit down after we had respectfully toasted the Queen who sadly was not expected to make an appearance.

"Can I finish my starter now?" Jet asked hungrily. Aware that she had not eaten since morning I knew she would not be amused when my reply was interrupted by further ear-splitting gavel bashing.

"The Commodore would like to take wine with anyone who has sailed around the world." I looked around expecting to see Ellen Macarthur but was even more surprised when the diminutive figure of one of the younger female members I had not seen for some time stood up proudly. We all toasted her incredible achievement before sitting back down albeit only briefly.

This eccentric performance continued with everyone desperately trying to time taking mouthfuls of food so as to avoid standing up looking like an over indulgent hamster. I voiced my concern to Jet as to the adverse effects this would have on the older reveller's digestive systems. Struggling to shell a stubborn prawn before the next interruption Jet barely acknowledged my apprehension.

"The commodore would like to take wine with anyone who has called out the lifeboat this year." Oh no! This was an impossible dilemma. If I remained seated there would be some in the room who would be aware of my secret and condemn my deceit. Conversely if I stood up now the whole club would......oh fuck! As I had deliberated Jet had proudly stood up, glass of wine in hand, preparing to be toasted. As I tentatively rose next to my partner, my forced smile turned into a wide grin as to my relief I noted four other members already on their feet. Absolution was administered in the form of a hearty toast before we all sat down. Jet looked like she'd just won gold at the Olympics. Personally I was feeling more than a little emotionally drained and in need of another drink.

The club's race secretary and the commodore had now made their way purposefully towards a table at one end of the hall. This was laden with a large number of shiny trophies in various shapes and sizes. The first award was presented to a nervous looking gentleman who was applauded enthusiastically as he carried the trophy back to his table like a guilty magpie stealthily stealing shiny objects. After being presented with the next five trophies the same recipient had adopted a much more confident demeanour. As he shuttled back and forth for each presentation he now more accurately resembled a rather imperious blackbird feathering its nest.

The subsequent applause became less exuberant but no one seemed too surprised at this monopoly of racing success. Most of the boats at the club are slow and heavy and designed for comfortable cruising rather than relentless racing. Adorned with new sails and stripped down to the bare essentials our strutting peacock's vessel possessed an unsurpassable advantage.

"Michael Davis.' I was interrupted from by alcohol induced daze on unexpectedly hearing my own name.

"That's you!" Jet added somewhat pointlessly.

"Have I won something?" I asked stupidly as Jet began pushing me in the direction of the one trophy remaining on the table. I didn't recollect having won a race but all was to be revealed by the commodore as I stood next to him perplexed by my unexpected success.

"The Stopher-Bell race is a competition for two trophies," the club secretary informed us. "The Stopher is for larger yachts while the Bell trophy is for smaller boats. Ten boats took part in the race which took place in some pretty treacherous conditions. However there was only one boat competing for the Bell trophy and that boat's name was Zulu. Congratulations Michael on coming first in a field of one." As I received my prize and headed for the security of my table I couldn't help notice the glare of annoyance on the peacock's face. I blushed as the guests on my table offered their congratulations while Jet beamed with pride.

With the trophy presentation complete and the waiters having cleared away the remains of our meal some of the tables were moved to provide an impromptu dance floor. As the music system played some timeless classics Jet and I partied like it was 1999 one more time. The commodore had by now removed his tie and undone most of the buttons on his shirt and was demonstrating some pretty outrageous dance moves from Saturday Night Fever. As the music played on I hoped that at least one of the members present was a trained first aider.

CHAPTER 9 – LIFT IN

So here I was, dressed up in an ill-fitting hard hat and oil stained, not so high vis jacket, looking like Bob the Builder, drinking my third cup of tea before even contemplating my first job of the day. I felt a sense of warm, national pride that I was able to perpetuate this age old British tradition as I continued to discuss the appalling state of the economy with one of my co-workers.

After being rudely woken up at 5am by the inane melody that passed as the alarm on my mobile phone, I had driven down to the sailing club for a six o'clock briefing preceding the annual lift in of boats from their winter storage in the club's boatyard, where they were safe from the turbulent waters of the icy Thames.

Late in November, after we had all recovered from the duck supper, all the yachts are removed from the river and stored on dry land. This allows owners to carry out routine maintenance before they are returned to the Thames when the weather starts to improve in the spring. Some members are to be found eagerly tinkering about on their boats whatever the weather while others start substantial repair work only several days before the lift in date.

Even the sun had not yet risen on this cold mid-March morning as the new commodore issued us with useful advice on how to avoid being crushed by the incredibly heavy boats being moved by the crane. I was allocated to the ambiguously named landing team which I assumed would involve waving coloured paddle boards at the crane driver as he steered each boat along its final approach into the water. I hastily discovered that my function was to be far less sedentary than anticipated and that I would be climbing on and off boats to detach each one from the hook hanging from the jib of the crane. My sense of pride at being trusted with this most technical of tasks was short lived when a fellow team member informed me we had not been chosen for our brains but our ability to still command the use of most of our limbs. As I looked around at the aging club members I realised what he meant. While some were currently recovering from recent operations on hernias and worn out knees, others were restricted by hip replacements, heart bypasses and the inability to see more than two feet in front of them. All of a sudden I was able to empathise with Scrooge as he was visited by the ghost of Christmas yet to come.

As we left the warmth of the club house to brave the final icy grips of winter I was relieved I had taken the time to put on every item of thermal clothing I owned. I felt like 'pigs in blankets' as I waddled to the boatyard. The crane was still being manoeuvred into its optimum lifting position so it seemed the only thing left to do was to indulge in an early breakfast. A few of the members wives had kindly prepared egg and bacon rolls which were soon being washed down with yet more mugs of hot tea.

Eventually the first boat was lifted in and I jumped aboard to remove the slings which formed the cradle that was hooked up to the crane. However as we turned around expecting to receive further instructions we were surprised to see the other teams staring at us in an apparent state of shock.

"Get the slings back on," shouted the commodore as I suddenly realised I was getting closer to the water. The boat I was standing on was sinking and not being the skipper I did not feel it was my duty to go down with her. We reattached her to the crane as quickly as possible but it was too late. We jumped ashore and it was a sad sight to see this old yacht leaking water from bow to stern as she was lowered gently back onto dry land. This was a disastrous start to the day and with Zulu scheduled to be lifted in later I debated momentarily whether it had been a wise decision to invest my money in her. I was slightly reassured when informed that wooden boats of this particular design were liable to leak if not prepared properly and that fibreglass boats like Zulu would be unlikely to endure a similar fate.

Several boats were subsequently lifted in successfully before coffee and biscuits provided a welcome distraction and an opportunity for everyone to congratulate each other on a job well done. I imagined that the last few boats would have to be moved by candlelight.

The rest of the morning ran like clockwork. One team attaching boats to the crane, my team releasing them while another towed each one to their temporary mooring. All coordinated with military precision by the banks man who only occasionally barked venomously at someone for getting in the way, while the rest of us looked sheepishly at each other like naughty schoolboys.

"Don't be so fucking stupid!" The morning had been relatively devoid of any major altercations despite the generous number of chiefs telling myself and the other Indians what to do. Admittedly there had been some minor complaints regarding boats not being prepared, ladders not being moved quickly enough and the small number of folk who managed to be in perpetual conversation. However a row had spontaneously broken out between two of the members who shared ownership of a boat. While the rest of us looked on in mild amusement they could not agree on where the two slings were to be positioned to safely support their yacht. Fortunately time was immediately called on this particular disagreement as the lovely ladies who had been toiling in the kitchen all morning called us in for lunch.

After generous helpings of baked potato and chilli con carnie followed by apple pie and custard, several older members of the club settled down for an afternoon nap. Feeling a little sleepy myself it was with some reluctance that I headed back out into the cold. However this was expected to be the final session and Zulu was due to be lifted next.

It's quite surreal watching an object you become accustomed to seeing in the water suddenly flying through the air hanging from a crane. I watched nervously as her aerial descent returned her to the medium in which she belonged. I stepped on board to release her from the crane and for a moment all appeared to have gone without incident. The crane driver who had now been on the go for about eight hours without the benefit of copious amounts of Tetley's finest now made a slight error of judgment. As he lifted the chains clear of Zulu's mast he made the mistake of turning the crane's jib slightly too soon. This caused the chains to dislodge the wind vane at the top of the mast which plummeted towards earth like Cupid's arrow. Fortunately, as it collided violently with the top of my hard hat, I did not suffer the debilitating effect of falling in love with the first person I set eyes upon. This could have been a little embarrassing in a boatyard full of bearded sailors. However as Galileo had so ingeniously proved at Pisa all falling objects continue to accelerate at the same rate due to gravity and consequently the impact of this small mistake set of a near calamitous chain of events.

First, the impact caused me to drop to my knees and collapse prostrate in the cockpit of my boat. Second, Tim who was part of my team, being incensed by this apparent incompetence, proceeded to shout profanities at the crane driver. Looking indignant and more than a little cross the driver leapt out of his cab and for a moment looked as if he was about to land one on Tim. To my colleague's relief he stormed off to the club house instead muttering something about sailors and morons. Thirdly, one of the member's wives who had witnessed the accident jumped onto Zulu and proceeded to administer mouth to mouth. As I regained consciousness to be confronted with an unfamiliar woman's face pressed against mine I managed to utter the words, "Get off me woman. I've only had a bang on the head. And can you stop loosening my clothing before I die from hyperthermia."

"That's enough of this nonsense," came the sobering tones of the commodore. Like the cavalry arriving at a nearly lost battle he proceeded to take charge and issue a series of battle cries. "Call an ambulance. Tim, go and apologise for your rudeness and someone get Veronica into a cold shower."

With normal service resumed I was given the all clear by a paramedic while the final boats were returned to the water with the help of a pacified crane driver. Tim was given a warm cup of sweet tea to calm his nerves while Veronica was taken home by her embarrassed husband.

The boatyard was now strangely empty, ready to be filled with the dinghies and tenders that would transport eager sailors to their yachts during the months ahead. Most of the members left for the warmth and comfort of their homes while only a few of the more dedicated remained to tidy up. As the crane drove away from the club I reflected on a physically demanding but rewarding day and the anticipation of the adventures to be enjoyed in the sailing season ahead.

CHAPTER 10 - FACEBOOK

Facebook. It never ceases to amaze me what people are prepared to share on line. Intimate details concerning their private lives and mundane facts about their social life. Don't get me wrong. I enjoy keeping in contact with old friends and sympathise with people who delight in sharing photographs of their lives with their families. However, I am often convinced that social networking merely provides a battleground where users slug it out to persuade others that their lives are far more interesting than in reality they really are.

Despite my cynicism I conceded to joining the sailing club's Facebook group in order to stay informed of forthcoming events. I would not want to miss the sensational scoop that a rusty ladder was being replaced or the navigational newsflash revealing the installation of a new buoy in the Thames. Despite the generous amount of trivia being unnecessarily divulged in this way I continue to enjoy receiving notifications regarding the many facets of the club. I am always particularly impressed with the efforts of the club's training secretary whose raison d'etre appears to be making sure all members are working towards qualifications which will enable them to confidently skipper the Titanic.

However I was totally shocked by the revelation of one member who unbelievably considered it appropriate to divulge his status on such a public platform as BOATLESS! Did this person have no shame? Had he not anticipated the repercussions of such a monumental admission? To confess to not sharing your life with a boat when advancing in years would at best cause embarrassment, at worst result in ostracism from the club. I predicted the impending conjecture which would spread like wild fire. Which party had initiated the separation? Was there another boat involved? Had the boat been mistreated?

I resolved to never make the same mistake and chose not to comment on the status for fear of being dragged into the unpleasant debacle.

CHAPTER 11 – SAILING WITH JET

2012. The year the Olympics came to the United Kingdom. No, I had not been selected to represent the country in one of the many sailing events. However with many of the sporting venues being in London all leisure boats on the Thames were required to display a notice stating where they were based. All boat owners had also been warned that there would be an increased presence from both the police and the army on the river.

"Are you going away for a couple of weeks?" Richard asked as I added yet another bag to the dinghy which was already visibly overloaded.

"No, just down to the River Medway for a night," I replied. Richard looked on bemused as Jet and I jammed ourselves in between our luggage and embarked upon the hazardous journey to Zulu's mooring.

As we distributed the contents of Jet's luggage into every corner of Zulu's single cabin I realised that we would need the nautical equivalent of Dr Who's tardis if we were ever to succeed in getting her looking ship shape. Jet had come fully tooled up for some serious partying with hair drier, straighteners and disco ball despite the fact we had no mains electricity on board.

Within minutes of heading downriver our journey was interrupted by the roar of the engines on a large black rib approaching at high speed. As it pulled alongside, the occupants, all dressed in black army uniforms, eyed me suspiciously.

"How many people on board?" asked one of the armed soldiers. As I surveyed my little boat wondering how many refugees and terrorists they thought I could cram into a twenty-two foot yacht Jet emerged coyly from the cabin. Before I could offer some ill-advised sarcasm, Captain Kalashnikov's attitude mellowed. While Jet appeared to have been mysteriously hypnotised by the sight of a man in uniform a similar spell seemed to have been cast on the rib's crew by the vision of a beautiful woman on board a yacht. As I insisted on trying to explain our itinerary and its omission of any terrorist related activities it appeared that Kalashnikov was more concerned with gallantly apologising to my companion for interrupting her trip. I contemplated breaking the spell by deliberately throwing myself overboard but decided this dramatic gesture would at best go unnoticed and at worst considered Kalashnikov's good fortune. Fortunately the rib's VHF radio came to my assistance, blasting out orders to attend a more urgent matter further upriver – Probably someone's packed lunch lost overboard, I thought to myself. As the army disappeared in a cloud of spray from their powerful engines I attempted to re-establish my role as alpha male by setting the engine to full throttle and powering towards the ever-widening Thames estuary at an impressive five knots. We soon had the sails up in a steady breeze and as we passed Canvey Island and the impressive pier at Southend on Sea I wallowed in having Jet's undivided attention once again.

After a pleasant journey which treated us to the joy of seeing a pair of apparently disorientated porpoise making their way up the

Thames we arrived at Queenborough at the entrance to the River Swale.

"How are we going to get ashore?" enquired Jet.

"We can't!" I informed her abruptly. "We didn't bring the dinghy." Jet's look of blind panic quickly turned to one of steely determination.

"Right! There's only one way to deal with this. We'll have to hitch a ride to shore."

"Are you crazy? This isn't the M25." I replied exasperated. "You'll never manage to get off a boat by sticking your thumb in the air."

Just then, a middle-aged couple with their sea faring dog proceeded to pass our boat in a small engine powered tender.

"Hello there. Is there any chance you could give us a lift to shore?" Jet implored politely.

"No problem. Hold on there a while. I'll take my wife and the dog to the pontoon and then come back for you." I shrugged my shoulders in disbelief. From now on I was putting Jet in charge of all the travel arrangements.

After we had all arrived safely on dry land we walked into town with our good Samaritans. We informed them of our need for more petrol and they duly gave us directions to the local garage. After thanking them they suggested we join them in the local pub for a meal so they could return us to our boat later on. We accepted their kind offer and headed off in search of fuel.

By the time we found our way back to the pub where Sarah and John had arranged to meet us, it was already starting to get dark. Their sailing credentials were beyond dispute as we noticed the considerable impression they had already made on the landlord's stock of wine. With our appreciation of sailing and alcohol in common it was easy to warm to our new friends as we shared stories about the strange and unexpected things that had happened to us while afloat. The landlord served us some excellent food as we enjoyed the warm summer air sat in the beer garden under a clear sky and full moon.

As the pub closed its doors, we made our way back to the pontoon where John had left his dinghy. Rather like most car accidents apparently happen within half a mile of the owner's house, most sailors are aware that the majority of sailing accidents happen during that short journey between their yacht and the shore.

It's incredible how alcohol can make the impossible a mere formality. Fortunately, John did not listen to my foolhardy advice that his tiny dinghy could easily carry the four of us plus their pooch. Instead he wisely transported Jet and me back to our yacht without any life threatening incidents before returning for his wife and pet. As I struggled to unlock the boat Jet looked at me knowingly.

"What?" I pleaded.

"Just as well you didn't bring a dinghy or we'd be yet another RNLI statistic."

It was a clear, windless night and after some romantic star gazing I was looking forward to a peaceful night's sleep. However Zulu had other ideas. Every time I was close to nodding off she would suddenly develop another barely audible but infuriating rattle which try as I might I found I couldn't ignore.

After dragging myself out of a warm cabin for the tenth time I found I had used up every piece of spare rope on Zulu to secure all the offending items. With my mind eventually at rest that we were not about to drift off into the middle of the English Channel I curled up next to an oblivious Jet as the sun started to rise.

It seemed I had only slept for a few moments when Jet insisted I get up to admire what was a beautifully warm and still morning. Without the luxury of a heads (a toilet for the uninitiated) I discretely relieved myself over the side of the boat. For some inexplicable reason Jet felt unable to perform a similar task until I had fashioned what she called a privacy blanket out of an old spinnaker draped strategically over the companionway. With her modesty intact she was able to make use of a bucket which I swore to myself I would never use to wash in, or clean the dishes.

Deciding to have breakfast on route we released Zulu from the mooring buoy before the harbour master arrived to charge us for our brief visit. Motoring towards the Thames in the warm morning sun we felt like a water borne Thelma and Louise making our

75

speedy getaway. As a gentle breeze from the east developed we hoisted the sails and began our six hour journey home.

"Shit! The depth's dropped to two metres." Jet warned me. With cat like reflexes taking over I quickly pushed the tiller away from me so that we tacked abruptly away from the approaching mud bank. Lost in conversation both of us had neglected to monitor the digital display telling us the distance between the bottom of the boat and the seabed. How quickly things can go wrong on a boat we reminded ourselves as we determined to pay more attention for the remainder of the journey.

As we negotiated the numerous craft moored near our sailing club Jet armed herself with a boat hook in preparation for picking up our mooring buoy. With the guidance of her confident hand signals from Zulu's bow I steered us on our final approach like a very slow Tom Cruise piloting his jet in Top Gun.

"We're not getting any closer," warned Jet who was now lying uncomfortably on the deck with her head and arms hanging outside the guard wires. Confused, I checked the engine which was running without any visible problems. Next, I looked for a reference point on the riverbank which quickly confirmed that we were indeed making no progress but also, to my dismay, revealed that the tide was a long way out.

"Bugger! We've grounded the boat," I exclaimed. Optimistically I turned the engine to full power hoping we could plough through the final ten metres of mud between us and the buoy. The mud was having none of it!

"We're still not moving," Jet verified as she made her way back to the cockpit looking less than amused. The good news was that Zulu having twin keels meant that she would sit safely in the mud until the tide came back in. The bad news being the six hours before Zulu would float again. Fortunately Kevin was rowing past us having just finished doing some maintenance on his yacht. Resisting the urge to comment on our embarrassing predicament he instructed us to tie some long mooring lines together which he then used to attach us to the buoy.

"That will secure the boat when the tide comes in. You'll have to come back and pull the boat up to the buoy when it does. I'll bring your dinghy over so you can get back to shore," Kevin added helpfully.

So it was that at four o'clock the next morning, having convinced Jet how much fun it would be, that we rowed back to Zulu in the dark. Anyone watching us from the shore would have questioned our sanity as our tiny boat glided silently through the moonlit water of the Thames in the early hours well before sunrise. It was no great surprise that there were no shouts of concern or mockery as we carefully climbed aboard our boat. I pulled on the long rope we had improvised earlier so that Jet could pick our mooring lines up and finally attach us to the buoy. Resisting a familiar urge to take Zulu for an impromptu sail as the sun rose, I capitulated to my companion who pointed out she would like to get back to the warm comfort of her bed.

The next time I saw Kevin at the club I thanked him for his assistance and pointed out how embarrassed I was about grounding my boat.

"Everyone gets stuck on the mud sooner or later," he kindly reassured me. "The only people who don't are those that hardly ever go out sailing." I felt vindicated by this revelation and contemplated when my frequent use of Zulu would result in a similar blunder. I resolved not to tell Jet that future disasters were indeed inevitable, but maybe she already knew.

CHAPTER 12 – BEACHING ZULU

This definitely didn't feel right, aiming Zulu towards a shingle beach on the banks of the River Thames with the aim of intentionally grounding her! As I felt her twin keels dig into the sand I glanced around to check my surroundings and get my bearings. The small beach I was now stranded on lay in a small cove next to an old church in the middle of Gravesend. The pedestrians walking along the road which ran beside the river must have been assuming I had made some serious errors in my navigation to have ended up in my present undignified predicament. I tried to ignore several sets of well intentioned but mistaken parents who pointed me out to their children muttering something about a silly man and a ship wrecked boat.

So why had I carried out such a reckless manoeuvre? Was I suffering from a sudden onset of cabin fever or had I overindulged on Zulu's meagre supply of rum? Surprisingly the explanation was one of simple practicality and zealous competitiveness.

A few weeks earlier I had taken part in one of the club's cruiser races. Jet had accompanied me and as usual was full of misguided optimism that we could take first place. We had made one of our better starts crossing the club line in third position and were holding our own racing downriver towards the first mark on a beam reach. We rounded the large green buoy carefully and with a strengthening tide assisting us headed back up the Thames towards the upriver mark. It now appeared that we were not only losing ground on the leaders but that the boats following us were looking likely to overtake us imminently. Jet looked at me questioningly as I shrugged my shoulders confident that I was doing everything in my power to optimise Zulu's speed. The sails were trimmed to within an inch of their lives and the helm was as well balanced as a tight rope walker crossing the Grand Canyon. Should I start throwing unnecessary items overboard to lighten the load? Maybe, but not yet I thought until we rounded the second mark and headed back downriver against the now quite significant incoming tide.

"We're going backwards. Everyone else is passing us. What's going on?" I shared Jet's frustration but just as I considered throwing my presently less optimistic companion overboard I suddenly diagnosed the reason for Zulu's malaise.

"She's got a dirty bottom," I informed Jet.

"What?" she responded with a slightly distasteful look on her face.

"The growth of weed and barnacles on the hull of the boat is creating so much drag that we can't fight the tide," I explained with the subtlety of Stephen Hawkins describing time space continuum. Jet continued to look unimpressed. In a painful illustration of our unfortunate position the slowest boat at the club passed us helmed by a skipper struggling to contain his excitement to such an extent that he almost knocked his crew overboard. I decided it was time to abandon the race. As I put the engine on and prepared to lower the sails I swore that I would rectify the situation before the next race.

"Are you all right mate?" yelled a concerned voice from behind me. The skipper of the Tilbury ferry had diverted his course to thoughtfully check on my welfare. Either that or he was mistakenly worried that I was intending to steal some of his customers. I waved reassuringly, gave him a thumbs up and he headed off with his cargo of Essex bound passengers. Surprised that anyone had even noticed my strange nautical manoeuvre I was positively dumbfounded when next the VHF radio crackled into life.

"A sailing craft has grounded along the shore from the Port of London offices." The message from what appeared to be a passing motor boat was quickly repeated. I waited in vain for a response but either the PLA were tired of dealing with eccentrics from the local sailing club or they had all taken the day off to enjoy the good weather. With the prospect of a needless rescue attempt looking increasingly unlikely I decided to focus on the job I had come here to carry out.

Like a mother cradling her sleeping infant and lowering it gently into its cot, so the ebbing tide slowly rested Zulu on the exposed shingle beach. As the boat finally tilted back onto its rudder, I found myself at a precarious angle with Zulu's cabin resembling the aisle of a jumbo jet just after take off. Cooking and eating dinner later was going to be a task worthy of The Generation Game.

Before I could start work on cleaning Zulu's hull I needed to get off the boat. Fortunately I had remembered to bring a small ladder which I lowered over the side and tied to the guard rails. I climbed down clutching a garden hoe and was able to take my first look below Zulu's waterline. A fashionable grey beard worthy of a swarthy George Clooney covered the bottom of the boat. Motivated by visions of Zulu racing through the water winning race after race, I started vigorously removing the growth with my trusty hoe. I was abruptly brought back to reality by the ring tone on my phone and an enthusiastic Jet announcing she was on her way to join me for the evening.

I had promised her a romantic dinner for two on the boat as the sun set over the river. What actually transpired probably stretched my description a little. However Jet appeared to enjoy the short walk into town to buy fish and chips which we ate on our laps at a slightly uncomfortable angle while watching Harry Potter on a small laptop. All that remained for us to do was to get Zulu back to her mooring when the tide eventually came in. Fortunately The Chamber of Secrets goes on forever as dusk turned to night and we waited expectantly as the tide crept towards us. Finally the water reached Zulu and the dinghy I had towed, as we watched apprehensively from the perceived safety of Zulu's cockpit.

First came the dull throbbing from the engines of a passing ship. Next we saw the large waves heading towards us that the ship had created. Then the wash collided with our dinghy bouncing it back onto the beach, knocking its small outboard engine off the transom and depositing it unceremoniously on the waterline.

"Quick! Get your boots on," Jet demanded. "Don't bother tying the laces. There's another wave coming," she continued as I fumbled with the footwear I had unwisely removed in order to get comfortable while we watched Harry and his mates battling the one who can't be named. I stumbled down the ladder and grabbed the engine as the water receded. "Hurry! You don't have much longer," I was warned. With almost supernatural effort equal to any of Potter's evil battling exploits, I staggered the few metres up the beach just before the approaching water flooded the area I had rescued the engine from.

As the wash from the passing super tanker dissipated I secured the engine to the dinghy and climbed back onto Zulu with the only casualty being my rather soggy shoelaces. Had the passing ship been named Voldemort, I would not have been surprised!

Zulu started to shift uneasily on the beach as each passing minute gradually saw the water surrounding us get higher. We started the engine and turned on the navigation lights as she tipped forward and started to float. Suddenly I felt her move unexpectedly towards the church wall to the side of us. Time to go! Jet instinctively grabbed the boat hook and pushed against the wall as I put the engine in reverse and turned the throttle as far as it would go.

Heart pumping and adrenaline racing we backed into the river towards a couple of large mooring buoys which I knew were in deeper water. I eased of the engine, turned Zulu downriver and began the short passage back to the sailing club. After the exhilaration of our recent night time departure we could now savour the peaceful trip past the moored boats and a group of elegant swans apparently suffering from insomnia. Jet, armed with a boathook in one hand and a petzl attractively adorning her pretty forehead, attached Zulu safely back on her buoy as I motored slowly against the almost slack incoming tide.

"That was fun," Jet confided as she turned and blinded me with light from her petzl. "Can we do it again next year?"

"Only if Hermione can put a spell on you so you can see in the dark," I replied as I attempted to guide our dinghy between the mud banks leading to the club's pontoon with my perilously impaired vision.

CHAPTER 13 – SOLO RACE

A couple of weeks later I drove to the club confident that Zulu was now in optimum condition for the scheduled Saturday afternoon race but disappointed I had not managed to find anyone willing to crew for me. The three other skippers all seemed to have surplus crew but no one appeared willing to volunteer to join me. Had my reputation for flirting with near disaster permeated the entire club community? The strengthening wind presented some testing sailing conditions but with little alternative I made the decision to race single handed.

Conditions were actually ideal for racing Zulu alone; a bracing, westerly wind and an incoming tide. The race officer who would usually delight in setting a course which even a courageous Ellen Macarthur would find challenging had kindly opted for a straightforward three laps between the clubhouse and a buoy about a mile down the river. This meant I could sail downwind against the tide through the boats moored in the shallowest water without having to tack repeatedly to avoid a devastating collision which could end my race. The tide would be weakest here which could improve my speed by a mind numbing half a knot. I knew I would have to beat back up the river but with the tide in my favour I could use the width of the Thames with the only problem being the occasional enormous container ship heading for Tilbury to play chicken with. The final part of my plan for nautical world domination was to lift my outboard engine out of the water to reduce the drag on my boat. I was armed and ready with a couple of cheese and ham sandwiches and a flask of tea to sustain me. Let the battle commence!

I wrestled for pole position like a petulant formula one driver as the lights above the clubhouse signalled ten minutes to go before the start of the race. Feeling I would have considerably less acceleration than an adrenaline fuelled Lewis Hamilton it was imperative to cross the start line as soon after the ten minute countdown as possible. Juggling with my stopwatch I succeeded in pressing the start button while simultaneously steering the boat and adjusting the sails. I bet Lewis didn't need this many hands!

As all three lights went out I had positioned myself perfectly to cross the line with minimal delay, avoid crashing into my opponents and head towards the upriver mark on a close reach. I was more than a little surprised to round the mark in first place after overtaking Petminder, the fastest boat in the fleet, but equally all too aware that my competition was in hot pursuit. Before I had time to become too complacent, Petminder hoisted its colourful spinnaker and proceeded to pass me as we sailed relatively sedately through the moored boats. The couple of old guys on board grinned smugly while pouring themselves a drink as the young, female crew they had cunningly recruited rushed around their yacht doing all the tasks involving more exertion than pouring a gin and tonic. Frustrated I continued to watch their lead grow as we left the moorings and proceeded to cross the Thames towards the downriver mark. Aware that Petminder would have to take down the sail which had given them the downwind advantage

I prepared myself for a livelier but much more evenly balanced race back up the river.

Like a big cat stalking its helpless prey I was soon making up the distance on my foe. As I pulled the sheets in even tighter my boat heeled at a precarious angle while water sprayed over the foredeck and into my face. This was what real sailing was about and the nervous look on the faces of those on the boat in front as they looked over their shoulders strengthened my resolve to win my first race. With each tack the whites of their eyes became a little more visible but unfortunately I was not quite able to overtake them before we reached the upriver mark for the second time.

Up went the spinnaker hoisted energetically by the youthful crew member as my hope for a famous victory started to evaporate. Goose winging downwind I managed to prevent my adversary building up too much of an advantage before we approached the downwind mark again. I headed straight for the big, green buoy as Petminder veered off course and was clearly struggling to take down the sail which had kept them ahead of me so far. What a pity, I thought to myself as I rounded the mark, pulled my sheets in tight and headed off on a second exhilarating sail into the wind. Only this time I was in first place!

I was uncatchable on this leg but knew I could still lose the race if I was overtaken again on the last lap. In the absence of any crew to distract me I was able to focus entirely on keeping the sails trimmed precisely and steering the boat as accurately as possible. I had always been grateful to friends who had joined me as crew in the past but they would have inevitably hampered my efforts with a well meaning "Can we have some lunch now?" or an ill-timed "Which rope do I have to pull?" I recalled Spike having joined me for one race in some bad weather and at the vital moment when we needed to tack found he had zipped the rope he needed to pull inside his waterproof jacket. Unbelievable!

I rounded the upriver mark with a significant lead and then watched in surprise as Petminder did the same, sailed past the club and proceeded to pull her sails down. Had she given up? Had the race been shortened? I had no way of telling from the other boats, which were by now half a lap behind. Without having enough hands to call the clubhouse on the VHF radio I opted to complete the third lap regardless. I felt a bit witless when I observed the other boats similarly mooring up after only a second lap and realised the single light above the clubhouse probably meant the race had been reduced to two laps. If only I had read my club handbook!

Having moored up to Zulu's buoy I was picked up by the club's safety boat whose crew were ecstatic that I had confined the rarely beaten Petminder into second place.

"You can really sail that boat when you want to," one of the skippers said kindly.

"Did you hear us cheering you on?" asked his crew.

I bathed in the rare admiration for my sailing prowess until we reached the clubhouse.

"Enjoy your extra lap?" Petminder's skipper asked me sarcastically.

"I thought I'd take a lap of honour," I replied. "I'm glad they shortened the course. It would have been embarrassing if I'd overtaken you a third time!"

The clubhouse was far from full but those that were there erupted into laughter and I celebrated my triumph both on and off the water with a large, cold beer.

CHAPTER 14 – GRAVESHAM THAMES RACE

The lights on the front of the clubhouse signalled the start of another race and Zulu passed over the start line in a respectable third place. Eleven boats had entered the race to the Thames Barrier and I had persuaded Jet to crew for me with the promise of some breath taking sightseeing after the race, as we continued from the barrier up to our destination for the night at Limehouse Marina near the centre of London.

By now Jet had become more than just competent crew and with my growing knowledge of how Zulu responded in different sailing conditions our expectations were high. With a rising tide and a strong wind behind us it would be a fast but comfortable sail into the capital.

Two boats had wisely chosen to declare their spinnakers and very quickly started to pull away from the fleet. However as a bend in the river caused a change in apparent wind direction we saw the leading boat struggling with its powerful downwind sail. We looked on incredulously as it sailed dramatically of course with its large blue sail dragging in the water.

"We're gaining on them," Jet pointed out less than sympathetically as we identified that the two boats in front of us were also having to alter direction to avoid a collision. As the leading boat abandoned its spinnaker I'm sure there was the same adrenaline rush on each boat as we headed towards the Dartford Bridge with very little distance separating the first seven boats.

As the river altered direction near Erith, three boats surged ahead as Zulu continued to battle with another three competitors. Majestically, the river twisted its way into London and Zulu displayed her different characteristics as we repeatedly gained and lost ground on different points of sail.

After an intense but exhilarating three hours and with the Thames Barrier visible ahead of us, we spotted a couple of dedicated club members peering over the sea wall on the south shore waving the distinctive club flag which marked the finish line. Jet was now getting over excited as we were slowly gaining ground on the much larger boat in front of us but at the same time were also being caught up by the boat behind. To avoid changing direction and consequently slowing down we were forced to head across to the wrong side of the river. Anticipating an imminent telling off from the Port of London Authority we crossed the finish line in a satisfying fifth place. Although we had regrettably not quite caught up with the boat in front, to our delight neither had we been overtaken.

With the serious matter of the race dealt with we started the engine and lowered the sails. Motoring thorough the Thames Barrier, Jet took the opportunity to pose for so many selfies it felt as if I had accompanied her on some exotic photo shoot. I was relieved that I no longer needed the assistance of my photogenic crew as we passed the captivating backdrops of the O2, Greenwich University, the Cutty Sark and the towering buildings housing the financial institutions around Canary Wharf.

Eventually we reached the marina where the Thames clippers rushing to deliver passengers to their destinations along the river had caused the water to become quite choppy. Motoring into the incoming tide to halt our progress we bounced around uncomfortably while waiting for our turn to enter the lock at Limehouse Marina. As we crept into the lock I edged slowly towards one side so that Jet could put a rope around a ladder near the bow of the boat. Anticipating her succeeding in doing this I straightened the boat so that I could secure us in a similar fashion at the stern. Things had obviously been going too well. I had turned before Jet could reach her target and now Zulu was drifting towards the yachts tied up on the other side of the lock. Jet didn't need to say anything. Her withering look told me she was not impressed. We would have been surprised and a little disappointed if there had not been lots of conflicting advice shouted at us but fortunately the guys on the boat we were drifting towards calmly took our ropes and tied us up to them. Another disaster averted!

Entering Limehouse Marina is like passing through a gateway to another world. Not quite a worm hole leading from a black hole in a sci-fi movie or a yellow brick road leading to Oz. However it is an oasis surrounded not by palm trees but tall apartment blocks and incredibly at one end the Regent's Canal provides a link with over two thousand miles of navigable canals around the country.

If we had expected to be able to throw our ropes to someone ashore we were to be disappointed. Most of the crews who had entered the basin before us were now preoccupied with the more urgent task of consuming the vast quantities of alcohol they had brought with them. I deliberated on how the extra weight they had been carrying had not resulted in an easy victory for Zulu. Just as Jet was poised to jump athletically onto a pontoon someone staggered towards us, beer in hand, and helped us moor up.

After catching up with how the other crews had fared in the race and taking a refreshing shower everyone ended up in the bar where we ate a delicious meal and continued to drink until late. While Jet and I paced ourselves a lot of the club members continued to overindulge and predictably the room got louder and louder. Jet offered a weary looking Kevin a drink which he declined reporting that he had probably had enough. Jet thoughtfully fetched him a portion of cheesecake instead which the following day he said he remembered eating but curiously couldn't recall how it had arrived on his table. After the meal most of the crews gathered on a couple of the larger yachts and the sound of laughter echoed around the marina until the early hours. To my horror Jet found herself in conversation with Peter, one of the more senior members of the club. He was enjoying recounting stories of near disaster including broken masts, missing rudders and torn sails. He had obviously survived these numerous incidents through a combination of knowledge, skill and good fortune. Jet determined to refer to him henceforth as 'wise man Pete.'

High water the next day meant a painfully early start at seven. Returning from the showers I passed several people who were barely able to walk, let alone sail. A pointless "How are you feeling?" was greeted with a remorseful nod. In stark contrast a sprightly looking Jet had already prepared a cooked breakfast and organised the boat for leaving. I vowed to make sure no one ever stole my capable crew.

We entered the lock uneventfully this time and watched disapprovingly as the crew of another boat struggled to tie her up. As the lock gates opened we slowly descended to the level of the Thames and waited for the instruction from the lock keeper to proceed. Clunk! As I put Zulu's outboard engine into forward gear it instantaneously stopped. Desperately I started the engine several more times and repeated the procedure with the same result.

"Anyone know anything about outboard engines?" I enquired hopefully. This time there was no advice shouted at me from the other boats in the lock.

"It might be the fuel filter," the lock keeper suggested which would have been helpful if I'd had any idea where the fuel filter might be. Like good Samaritans, Christian and Victoria who were also in the lock, shouted that they were happy to give us a tow. As the only viable alternative was being condemned to go up and down in the lock for a hellish eternity I accepted their generous offer.

Once out into a much more tranquil River Thames our friends proceeded to tow us downriver in the absence of any wind in which we might sail. Jet put the kettle on as we conceded that at the speed we were going there would be a lot more tea consumed before we arrived at Gravesend. Victoria was on a similar wavelength but discovered she had no milk. Disaster! However in a manoeuvre worthy of the green berets Jet used the boathook to pass a carton between the boats as Christian shortened the tow line to close the gap separating us.

Numerous cups of caffeine infused tea and enough chocolate bars to bring on a diabetic attack later the wind started to fill in from the east. Christian started to turn around to check on us more frequently and I could tell from the impatient look on his face that he was eager to do some sailing. Jet on the other hand, had other ideas.

"Why can't he tow us all the way back to the club?" she pleaded when I informed her that I was going to have a chat about releasing the tow rope. I knew she was nervous about attempting the rest of the journey without the security of an engine. I, on the other hand, was secretly relishing the opportunity to put my sailing skills to the test. Reluctantly Jet agreed to sail home and we threw the rope across to our friends.

With the wind strengthening it was inevitably going to be an impromptu race back to the club. Our two yachts raced neck and neck on an exhilarating beam reach until I was forced to tack to avoid colliding with a freight ship moored at Tilbury docks.

Christian and Victoria pulled away from us as we rounded the last turn in the river before the familiar skyline of Gravesend came into view. Jet looked nervous and asked "How are we going to get the sails down and moor up without an engine?"

"Trust me," I replied confidently. "We'll heave to in the middle of the river, get the mainsail down and sail up to our mooring using just the genoa." I'm unsure whether I'd totally impressed Jet or baffled her with jargon but she followed my instructions and we secured ourselves to our mooring buoy without any calamity.

"This sailing lark is easy," I boasted as we tidied up the boat in preparation to go ashore.

"Yes, but remember the sea is a cruel mistress," Jet reminded me with a smile as I lifted the broken engine out of the water. It was at this moment that I discovered what had caused the engine to fail.

"The good news is that we don't need a new engine," I explained to Jet cheerily. "The bad news is that we could have used the engine to get back if we'd spotted the carrier bag wrapped around the propeller."

Jet was speechless as I removed the offending item but as we were ferried to shore by the club's trot boat I was proud to hear her describing how we had safely managed the journey home and attached Zulu to our buoy with only our sailing skills to aid us.

CHAPTER 15 – KNOWLEDGE AND NOSH

How shallow are those who try to impress by offering their services against their better judgement. How foolish had I been to agree to give an instructional talk at the sailing club at one of their monthly 'knowledge and nosh' sessions.

In my defence I had assumed all details of my misguided volunteering would be quickly forgotten or discarded in preference of some more weighty topic. However several months after a casual conversation with the perpetually enthusiastic club secretary my name had appeared on the club website with a date confirming my contribution to the social calendar. Like a prisoner on death row I understood the finality of knowing the instant of one's fate but without the luxury of comprehending that I would not recall the experience.

I had decided on the title of my presentation. The 'physics of sailing'. That ought to be intimidating enough to put most people off. With any luck the UK's unpredictable weather would conspire to prevent a few more attending. Who was I kidding? The club's church like interior would probably be more crowded than a Billy Graham sermon. Without Billy's fanaticism inducing charisma the trick would be to keep my audience sufficiently occupied to distract them from the mediocrity of the content.

"I need the help of a couple of glamorous assistants," I announced trying desperately not to sound like Bruce Forsythe. As the assembled audience consisted mainly of men over fifty it was not difficult to pick out Jet and her new best friend, Victoria. I dare not contemplate the consequences of having selected anyone other than Jet. At best she may have sabotaged my presentation; at worst I may have never seen her again.

I set Victoria and Jet to work handing out cards to the bemused gathering while I attempted to explain the task as simply as possible. "The cards either state a scientific principle related to sailing, a description of a principle or a picture illustrating a principle." The silence in the room made me wonder if I was speaking a foreign language and certainly did not fill me with confidence that I was making myself understood. I continued. "The objective is to talk to people in the room until you have formed a group of three with cards related to the same scientific idea." I felt encouraged by some earnest nodding as everyone got to their feet and started mingling.

As I started preparing the next task I wondered whether ultrasound, upthrust and the Bernoulli principle would have everyone walking around in circles for hours. However as I contemplated whether I should have advised bringing sleeping bags and a light breakfast to the event the task appeared to have been completed. The chaotic melange of chattering bodies had transformed into neat groups of three waiting expectantly for my next instructions. I had the groups proudly read out their cards to confirm they had identified the connections correctly as it dawned on me that a group of well read sailors would collectively have a vast general knowledge. Not surprisingly they had solved my little problem more quickly than I had anticipated.

"Your next task is to work in pairs to construct a boat. The boat which can carry the most weight will win the challenge." As everyone looked around the room for the wood, fibreglass, rope and shackles they assumed that I had concealed in the club I reached into a small bag I had brought with me. I suspected my audience were more than a little under whelmed when I proceeded to hand out fist size lumps of brown plasticine. Despite their immediate disappointment each team instantly began conferring as to how to transform the child's plaything they had been given into something resembling the QE2. I had succeeded in engaging my audience through the thinly disguised deception of introducing the element of competition.

As I supervised the building work like an over zealous exam invigilator I started to wonder if anyone in the room had actually noticed the shape of the boats moored only a short distance away in the river. None of the yachts I could see through the window resembled the miniature pancakes, doughnuts and bathtubs being fashioned enthusiastically before me. I resisted the growing urge to intervene.

With the fifteen minute time limit I had set having expired the teams carefully carried their strangely diverse creations over to a table where I had filled a large washing up bowl with water. As the pancake was confidently placed in the water by Jet and her partner, I just had time to place a single pound coin on top before it sank gracefully below the surface, weaving its way to a rather shallow Davy Jones' locker. The room filled with tension as everyone deliberated whether to laugh or commiserate. Jet looked resigned to losing the competition until the next pair presented their handiwork. Disturbingly the shape of the plasticine had not been altered and as the oblong mass was lowered into the water predictably it sank immediately. Tragic! Everyone looked bewildered as the evening's two youngest participants explained that they didn't like the weird, sticky feel of the modelling clay. I decided to move on swiftly.

After the doughnut had managed to support, if rather precariously, the grand total of two pound coins I sensed that everyone's expectations had risen considerably. Finally it was the turn of the bathtub lovingly shaped by Christian and Victoria, a couple who Jet had discovered had romantically met as a result of joining the club. I can only imagine they had been listening to unchained melody in their earpieces as they sculpted this masterpiece together. There was an audible gasp of euphoria as the ninth pound coin was delicately placed in the vessel. Christian, standing proudly behind Victoria, wrapped his arms around her. Was that the Righteous Brothers I could still hear? Would their boat hold ten coins? Would we ever get to enjoy the promised nosh at the end of the evening? As I held up the tenth coin like a treasured holy grail our questions were answered. Before I could add the coin the bathtub tilted to one side, water spilling over the rim, before joining the other plasticine wrecks at the bottom of the bowl.

After some well deserved applause for our winners I concluded with a brief explanation of Archimedes's principle. I pointed out that the upward force supporting the boat could be optimised by increasing the weight of water being displaced by the plasticine. As eyes started to glaze over I finished off with a succinct "Make the boat as big as possible and it's more likely to float," before introducing the finale to my act. The quiz!

It was now approaching eight o'clock in the evening and after the exertion of the first two tasks everyone was in need of some sustenance. Thanks to the dedication of Hannah, the club secretary, and a few keen volunteers there were several dishes of home made lasagne slowly cooking in the club's galley. It was decided that the food would best be served before anyone collapsed from malnutrition and that we could conduct the quiz while enjoying the much anticipated meal.

I proceeded to hand out quiz sheets while endeavouring to avoid the stampede to get served in the kitchen. Seeing that I was consumed by my determination to make sure that no one missed out on participating in the quiz Jet kindly brought me a plate of the steaming hot lasagne to where we were sitting. Each quiz sheet contained ten questions related to the scientific concepts I had alluded to during the course of the evening. Rather like a teacher, with over optimistic expectations, I hoped to discover if through my efforts I had indeed succeeded in imparting any knowledge whatsoever to my class.

With everyone's appetite well on the way to being satisfied the teams started deliberating the questions I had presented them with. Unfortunately some of the quiz sheets had fallen victim to some careless use of the club's cutlery and I was asked to interpret more than a few words almost completely obliterated by stubborn tomato sauce stains.

When each team had given the quiz their best shot the sheets were exchanged and I asked each pair to give an answer to one of the questions. After a lengthy marking process during which each team jealously guarded their varying degrees of success, the scores were in. Like the host of numerous celebrity reality TV shows I nurtured the growing tension by announcing the top three scores in reverse order. Despite the crunching of garlic bread, scraping of forks on virtually empty plates and hissing of opening beer cans I could sense everyone on the edge of their seats by the time I announced the winner. Simon was so overwhelmed by his success that he downed his drink, insisted his wife grab her coat and left to get an early night.

I had succeeded in pulling it off despite my trepidation. As several participants thanked me and pointed out how much they had learnt from the evening I felt a growing sense of having accomplished my aim to educate and amuse a potentially critical audience. Maybe after a few drinks and a bit of intervention from Jet I could be persuaded to do a repeat performance next year.

CHAPTER 16 – A CHANGE OF LIFESTYLE

It had been almost ten years since Spike had suggested we participate in a local dinghy sailing course which had been the spark that had opened up a whole new world to Jet and myself. I had a lot to be grateful to Spike for. I would have left him Zulu in my will if he hadn't already told me he didn't want her.

"Not everyone is obsessed with sailing," Jet informed me dispassionately. I found this both a shock and almost impossible to believe.

We had both enjoyed numerous adventures and made some lifelong friends as a result of discovering a world which is hidden to those not involved in the sport. Zulu was now our second home. The Thames, from Tower Bridge to the daunting expanse of the estuary, was now our back garden which we had become familiar with racing and cruising on. On sailing holidays in the Mediterranean, we had anchored off deserted islands and admired spectacular sunsets. We had negotiated dangerous reefs in the Caribbean during the hurricane season. We had miraculously survived violent storms in Thailand which had dissipated to reveal deserted, golden beaches.

We had also been welcomed by a whole community at the sailing club with whom we had wined and dined and far too often over indulged. On the considerate advice of longer standing members who were concerned that I was incapable of consuming the vast quantities of alcohol required of a serious sailor, I would go into training several days before each social event. Despite the potential calamitous effects on my liver, this involved drinking increasing amounts of beer, wine or spirits over several days leading up to an occasion. This ensured I had the stamina necessary to tolerate the demanding rigors of a whole evening's club festivities. Training for football in my youth had never been this tough.

It was during one of our sailing trips to the Med when Jet and I had a conversation which was to lead to the next chapter in our lives together. We had chartered a comparatively small yacht in one of the Greek marinas near Athens. I say comparatively because whatever size boat we hired it seemed that wherever we moored or anchored all the other yachts that joined us in each location would always be at least six foot longer. I had given up trying to uncover a reason for this conspiracy and had instead elected to choose the cheapest boat which inevitably would be the smallest. We were anchored in a small, crescent shaped bay with a narrow, sandy beach surrounded by pine trees. The sun was setting as we listened to music while preparing an evening meal. Dressed in shorts and t-shirts our skin was still warm in the heat of the Mediterranean summer.

"This is another magical moment," I whispered to Jet as she wiggled her hips in time with the music while expertly chopping some tomatoes. I was reminded of our first trip together when she had first demonstrated her ability to multitask so skilfully.

"Yes, I know," she agreed. "It's so perfect here. I really don't want to go home."

I understood exactly what she meant as I expect would anyone who has not wanted their two week summer getaway to end.

"It's not a holiday we need, it's a change of lifestyle," I clarified.

Jet nodded knowingly. She had heard me say this on numerous trips but of course our dream always came to an end, we had left our temporary paradise and returned home to work and routine. However, this time my observation would be supported with a cunning plan. Baldrick would be proud.

"I've been thinking," I continued. Jet resisted the obvious disparaging response. "We both have money we've worked hard to save. We could sell Zulu and have enough money to buy a yacht in the Med and survive for a couple of years. What do you think?"

"I think you're mad, but that doesn't come as a surprise. Where would we go? What would we do in the winter?" Jet would understandably have more questions that would need answering.

"We could buy a boat in northern Croatia, sail down to Greece and then across the Cyclades to Turkey." I suggested confidently. "When the weather turns we can shelter in a marina and hook up to mains electricity to power a couple of fan heaters." Was my enthusiasm going to convince Jet that this was a brilliant proposition?

Knowing she would be concerned about missing friends and family I continued. "People can fly out and join us for parts of the journey. With only flights to pay for I'm sure we'll be inundated with prospective guests."

Jet smiled as she served the meal we had prepared. I poured a couple of generous glasses of local wine and we continued our conversation over dinner.

In fact we continued our conversation long into the night. Long after the wine had run out and the CD had replayed itself for the fifth time Jet agreed it was an idea worth considering. We resolved to continue the discussion after the holiday when we were more likely to take a more rational approach to the questions we would need to answer. Miraculously it even occurred to us that it might be prudent to debate such a significant change to our lives when we weren't both very drunk.

And so it was that after much armchair deliberation we found ourselves walking through arrivals at Pula airport in northern Croatia just as the weather was starting to improve in early April. We had previously found a suitably equipped yacht in the area and had flown out to check it over. It had been just what we were looking for. Large enough to live on comfortably but not so big as to make it difficult for two people to handle in marinas and small harbours. We had paid for it and spent a few days tidying her and doing routine maintenance before flying home to finalise our affairs in England.

It was a fifteen minute taxi ride from the airport to the marina during which we tried hopelessly to make conversation with our driver. We were both understandably distracted by the feeling of excitement and apprehension as we drove through the parched trees towards the turquoise blue of the Adriatic coast.

"Do you remember the first time we boarded a boat together?" Jet asked me as we prepared to step onto what would be our home for the foreseeable future.

"Oh yes," I replied. "You had no idea what you were letting yourself in for and I had no idea what I was doing."

"But we survived that and a lot more since despite the fact you never know what you're doing," Jet teased.

"Well I can't promise you that nothing will go wrong but I'm pretty sure I can guarantee it will be an adventure," I offered.

"Oh I know it will be fun, eventful and never boring. But the sea can be such a cruel mistress!" she reminded me.

Later as the stars lit up the night sky and the water gently danced around the ships waterline we crawled into our warm bed knowing our lives had changed forever.

GLOSSARY

Antifoul – paint which reduces growth of barnacles on boat's hull

Beam – side of boat

Beam reach – sailing with wind coming over side of boat

Beat – continually zig zag when sailing into the wind

Boom – metal spar attached to bottom of sail

Bow – front of boat

Cleat – device used to secure rope to

Cockpit – outside seating area

Companionway – steps leading to boat's interior

Ebbing – tide going out

Foredeck – outside area at front of boat

Furl – roll up a sail

Galley – kitchen

Genoa – sail at front of boat

Guard wire – wire at side of boat which prevents falling overboard

Halyard – rope which pulls up a sail

Hatch – sliding cover to companionway

Heave to – stop the boat using sails and tiller

Helm – steering wheel

Keel – metal structure on bottom of boat

Pilotage – visual references to guide a boat

Ready about – skippers signal to indicate a change of direction

Saloon – seating area inside boat

Spinnaker – large sail for sailing downwind

Stern – rear of boat

Tack – turn the front of the boat through the wind

Tender – small boat powered by oars or small engine

Tiller – handle which is used to steer the boat

Winch – used to pull ropes when a large force is needed

THE AUTHOR

Michael Davis is a school teacher living in Kent. He loves to travel, trying to fulfil his ambition to visit every continent. He plays the guitar and sings and has played at music venues around the country including the Rock Garden in London. His love of sport involves him in playing football, basketball and golf in his more sedate moments. He caught the sailing bug late in life, initially in dinghies, and now owns a small yacht moored on the River Thames. He tries to charter a yacht in a new destination each year and hopes to spend a prolonged period sailing around the Mediterranean in the future.

Printed in Great Britain
by Amazon